Ghost
Sudoku

Kaye Morgan

BERKLEY PRIME CRIME, NEW YORK

THE BERKLEY PUBLISHING GROUP
Published by the Penguin Group
Penguin Group (USA) Inc.
375 Hudson Street, New York, New York 10014, USA

Penguin Group (Canada), 90 Eglinton Avenue East, Suite 700, Toronto, Ontario M4P 2Y3, Canada
(a division of Pearson Penguin Canada Inc.)
Penguin Books Ltd., 80 Strand, London WC2R 0RL, England
Penguin Group Ireland, 25 St. Stephen's Green, Dublin 2, Ireland (a division of Penguin Books Ltd.)
Penguin Group (Australia), 250 Camberwell Road, Camberwell, Victoria 3124, Australia
(a division of Pearson Australia Group Pty. Ltd.)
Penguin Books India Pvt. Ltd., 11 Community Centre, Panchsheel Park, New Delhi—110 017, India
Penguin Group (NZ), 67 Apollo Drive, Rosedale, North Shore 0632, New Zealand
(a division of Pearson New Zealand Ltd.)
Penguin Books (South Africa) (Pty.) Ltd., 24 Sturdee Avenue, Rosebank, Johannesburg 2196,
South Africa

Penguin Books Ltd., Registered Offices: 80 Strand, London WC2R 0RL, England

This is a work of fiction. Names, characters, places, and incidents either are the product of the author's imagination or are used fictitiously, and any resemblance to actual persons, living or dead, business establishments, events, or locales is entirely coincidental. The publisher does not have any control over and does not assume any responsibility for author or third-party websites or their content.

GHOST SUDOKU

A Berkley Prime Crime Book / published by arrangement with Tekno Books.

PRINTING HISTORY
Berkley Prime Crime mass-market edition / January 2010

Copyright © 2010 by Penguin Group (USA) Inc.
Sudoku puzzles by Kaye Morgan.
Cover illustration by Trisha Krauss.
Interior text design by Laura K. Corless.

ISBN: 978-0-425-23262-0

BERKLEY® PRIME CRIME
Berkley Prime Crime Books are published by The Berkley Publishing Group,
a division of Penguin Group (USA) Inc.,
375 Hudson Street, New York, New York 10014.
BERKLEY® PRIME CRIME and the PRIME CRIME logo are trademarks of Penguin Group
(USA) Inc.

PRINTED IN THE UNITED STATES OF AMERICA

10   9   8   7   6   5   4   3   2   1

To the nieces, Maureen and Kathleen, Jacqueline and Caroline, who occasionally read some of this stuff. And of course many thanks to Michelle Vega of The Berkley Publishing Group, who, like it or not, has to edit it all.

"I've had good flights and bad ones on small planes," Liza Kelly said. "Looking at a view like this, I can see why you do it."

Seen from about 8,000 feet up in the air, the Pacific Ocean off Oregon looked like a huge, burnished, silver-blue shield.

"Yeah, well, the weather is pretty decent," Wish Dudek told her. "You might not say that if we were going through some turbulence."

"Been there, don't want to do that ever again," Liza replied. "It's like riding a roller coaster—only without the rails."

Wish chuckled, a sound that had become familiar to Liza over the past twenty-five years of TV watching. He'd hosted the game show *D-Kodas* long before Liza got into high school, much less started with the Markson Agency. Nowadays, Dudek was a client of the publicity agency where Liza was a partner, though this flight was the longest amount of time Liza had ever spent with him. For most of the trip they'd talked about Liza's other career as a syndicated columnist and creator of sudoku puzzles.

Wish had shown that he understood the rules of sudoku—fitting the numbers 1 through 9 into the rows and columns of a nine-by-nine grid based on twenty or so clues scattered around the matrix. What interested him were the possibilities of inserting information into the 81-space sudoku array. "Have you ever seen a sudoku puzzle that hid a message?"

"I've found various sets of numbers hidden in sudoku," she said. "But working with only the numbers one through nine—and having them only appear about twenty times per puzzle as clues—it's kind of tough to encode any extensive communication."

"And some of those puzzle makers had pretty intense reasons to pass a message along," Wish went on.

Liza sighed. Now her pilot had definitely pushed the conversation into what she grudgingly considered her third career. "Yeah, I've stumbled across some murders, and because I had a connection—and there were puzzles involved—I tried to do something."

"Like solving them," Wish said.

"It's not like cracking a sudoku," Liza warned, "or any of the puzzles on your show. Life is a lot messier, not to mention irrational."

"It's done well for you." Wish didn't look up from his instruments. "Between that and your column, you're almost a celebrity."

Liza rolled her eyes. "My partner had a lot to do with that."

Wish laughed. "When it comes to publicity, who in their right mind would go against Michelle Markson?"

"And as far as celebrity goes, can you guess how I spent the last two weeks?" Liza asked.

"Enjoying a vacation, judging from that tan."

"Going incognito." Liza gave a sour laugh. "Earlier this spring, I tried to mix some R and R with a sudoku tournament at a resort."

"I think I heard about that," Wish said. "People started turning up dead."

Liza nodded. "So this time instead of going as Liza Kelly, I went as Mrs. Michael Langley, using a credit account Michael and I hadn't closed when we started divorce proceedings."

"Heard about that, too." Wish glanced over. "So is it final yet?"

Liza shook her head, unwilling—or maybe unable—to answer. How could she explain three men in her life—including an almost-ex-husband?

Instead, she took a shot at changing the subject. "Anyway, I got two weeks of sun, surf, and spa treatments. No sudoku, no cell phone—"

"No celebrity," Wish finished for her with a lopsided smile. "Not that I can tell you much about that. When we're shooting, I'm doing five to six shows a day, locked in the studio." He tapped his cheek. "They spray this tan on me."

The sense of humor that always kept popping up on the screen raised its head, transforming his conventionally handsome face with an impish grin. "Guess I can't complain, though. I had an Irish mother who named me Aloysius and a Polish father who made me swear I'd never abandon the proud Dudek name. With all that, it's a miracle I made it anywhere in show business."

That got a laugh from Liza. "Hey, you did well enough to buy your own airplane."

"Just a two-seater—barely a puddle jumper."

Liza cast an apprehensive glance at the ocean far below.

"But it gives me the freedom to move around and make some use of my nationally syndicated name." Wish flashed that grin again. "I'm not just flying up here to give you a lift, you know."

"That's right," Liza said. "Michelle mentioned you were going to a political dinner."

"Up in Seattle." Wish's irrepressible grin grew wider. "I'm afraid my political views may not fit in with most Hollywood types. But I try to make myself useful when I'm asked. Put my famous, funny-looking face front and center for a good cause."

He shot Liza a speculative look. "Have you ever considered politics? I'm guessing your hometown is probably the same size as Wasilla—"

"Oh, please," Liza replied quickly, to cut that idea off. "As if I don't have enough going on in my life right now, you'd have me leap into an election campaign."

She smiled. "I guess the best thing I can do is to quote Michelle: 'From the time I started doing PR, I got a belly-ful of deceit and megalomania from my first clients in the entertainment business. So I drew the line at politicians.'"

Wish laughed so hard, Liza had a moment's panic at whether he was going to plunge them into the ocean so far below. "I've got to steal that," he finally said when he had himself under control. "Maybe I can work it into tonight's after-dinner speech."

"Well, in this case, I don't think Michelle would be interested in attribution," Liza told him. "Especially since this isn't a show biz crowd."

Still chuckling, Wish banked the plane, and Liza sucked in her breath as the seacoast came into view. All of a sudden, she was home. The view spread before them was the same as the map of Killamook County from her fourth-grade classroom, except that now she got to see that map transformed into the real world.

There was the indentation of Maiden's Bay, as if some titanic being had poked into the coastline and then curved its finger. At the mouth of the inlet, a peninsula jutted into the water, sheltering a harbor. That was the township of Maiden's Bay, Liza's childhood hometown. Farther along, beyond the curve of the bay, she could make out the town of Killamook, the county seat. And in between the two, on the northern shore of the bay, was Killamook Airport. That was a rather grand name for a runway attended only during daylight hours.

After speaking on the radio, Wish brought the plane in for a landing. He helped Liza disembark, handed out her luggage, and then taxied off. As soon as flight control gave the okay, he was airborne again, off to Seattle.

Liza, however, still had miles to go before she got home. And her car was where she'd left it after sneaking out of town—in the long-term parking lot at Portland Airport. She reached into her shoulder bag to call for a cab—and then pulled a face when her cell phone didn't light up.

Great, she thought, *the battery died somewhere during my travels.*

Jamming the phone back in the bag, Liza tried to remember if she'd noticed a pay phone anywhere around the scatter of buildings surrounding the tarmac. Just as she began to give up hope, a voice called her name.

Liza turned to see Jimmy Perrine waving his battered Stetson. His long salt-and-pepper hair was pulled back in a scruffy ponytail, and he wore a Hawaiian shirt in nearly radioactive colors. "That plane you rode in on wasn't much better than my crate."

Jimmy had piloted her a time or two. Essentially, he was happy to fly just about anywhere as long as his passenger paid for the fuel.

Liza decided to try her luck and ask if Jimmy would do the same for ground transportation. He actually agreed to take her to Maiden's Bay without even asking for gas money. She climbed into the cab of his pickup after stowing her bags in the back, and off they went.

As they took the highway along the coast, the bay looked almost supernaturally blue and pretty, as if it were posing for photographers from the state tourism bureau. Liza wasn't taken in by the view of the sun on the waters—she'd crawled along the road in dense fog and seen the bay lead gray with whitecaps torn by blizzardy winds. Still, she decided to take advantage of the nice weather, rolling down the window—something she hadn't been able to do on Wish's plane.

"Haven't seen you around lately," Jimmy said as they drove along. He glanced back at the luggage in the truck bed. "Guess you were traveling."

"Just taking a break," Liza told him. "This is the time of year for it, right?"

He nodded. "Guess so. Saw your face on TV, though."

Liza grimaced. After that wild and woolly case at the sudoku tournament, *she'd* gotten sick of seeing her face on the box. "With luck, that should all be over by now."

"Think so?" Jimmy glanced at her in surprise and seemed about to say something more.

"That's the way I'd like it," Liza said.

Jimmy just shrugged and turned back to the road. Liza dragged out her defunct cell phone and examined it. "Damned useless thing."

"Not working?"

"And I don't know why," Liza fumed. "I haven't had it on since I left town."

"Oh," Jimmy said. "Ah. So you haven't talked to anybody round here for what—a week?"

"Two," Liza said.

For some reason, Jimmy seemed to find that funny. But then, he had a strange sense of humor. Liza put it down to his spending too many hours flying high in the sky, or his Jimmy Buffet approach to life. But Perrine seemed to find a laugh in a lot of things most folks wouldn't consider funny. "You may find some changes," he said with a smothered chuckle.

Liza laughed. "Come on, Jimmy. Nothing ever changes in Maiden's Bay. What happened? Did they finally open some stores by the new boardwalk?"

"You'll see for yourself soon enough," Jimmy replied. "I wouldn't want to ruin the surprise." He looked as if he were about to start laughing, but then smoothed out his face and concentrated on his driving.

As they came up on the exit for Maiden's Bay, Liza asked if Jimmy could just drop her off downtown. She was friendly with several shopkeepers who wouldn't mind watching her bags while she bought some supplies and took them home. Then maybe she could borrow the car from her neighbor Mrs. Halvorsen . . .

A tinny rendition of "The Washington Post March" interrupted her mental planning. Liza looked up to find a float done up in red, white, and blue bunting parked next to the war memorial—and blocking the traffic circle around that piece of uninspired statuary.

Liza sighed. She hated the unimaginative tone of political theater in general, and the local nonsense in particular offended her professional publicity sense.

A bunch of people holding clipboards milled around the street and sidewalks, holding out pens to both motorists and passersby. Some of them wore those awful make-believe straw boaters made of polyfoam.

Of course, the hats boasted red-white-and-blue bands, probably emblazoned with the would-be candidate's name.

Just as she was squinting to make out the print, a voice booming over the loudspeakers distracted her.

"Step right up, voters of Maiden's Bay!" The pitch sounded better suited for a carnival sideshow than a political rally. "Put your names on our petitions to nominate the town's next mayor . . . Liza Kelly!"

2

The world seemed very far away, as if Liza were peering at it through the wrong end of a telescope. A roaring in her ears drowned out both the pitchman's voice and John Philip Sousa. She also felt her head pounding in time to her elevated heartbeat.

Is this what it feels like to have a stroke? a detached part of her brain asked with interest.

Then the world snapped back into focus. Liza found herself out of Jimmy's pickup and stalking up to the float. No, this wasn't a stroke. It was pure fury. She wished she had something in her hands, a baseball bat—no, a sledgehammer—to bash the bunting off the float, crush those bullhorns, maybe brain a couple of those clipboard-wielding idiots . . .

"Liza! Here you are!" A jubilant voice penetrated the red fog that had rolled in to cloud Liza's vision. She turned to discover her neighbor Elise Halvorsen bearing down on her.

Mrs. H.'s round, plump face was wreathed in smiles. Liza noticed her neighbor wore her best summer-weight hat, a wispy stray number whose wide, fluttery brim always looked like a pair of wings trying to lift the hat off the woman's head and into flight. Mrs. H. had decorated her chapeau with one of the red-white-and-blue hatbands. Her hat was smaller than those plastic monstrosities, however, so the slogan read, KELLY FOR MAYO.

Liza found the idea of becoming a condiment so ridiculous that she couldn't help laughing. "Good to see you, Mrs. H. And how have you been?"

"Busy," her neighbor replied. "I guess it was two days after you left that Clark came around with a petition. I jumped in at once, helping, and I haven't looked back since."

"So this Clark is running things?" Liza said.

Mrs. H. nodded. "Clark Hagen."

"He must be around here somewhere—this Clark Hagen—right?" Liza tried to keep the tone light, but she could hear a clash like iron in her voice as she repeated the name.

"He should be." Mrs. H. looked around in perplexity. "I wonder where he got to?"

When Liza scanned the crowd, she noticed that since her arrival—or maybe since Mrs. H. had called out her name so loudly—all the clowns in the fake straw hats had vanished.

Looks like the phonies in the phony hats were the hired professionals, Liza thought. Now the other folks with clipboards—volunteers like Mrs. H.—looked around uncertainly.

Liza walked up to the front of the float, to the truck that pulled it, only to find the door open and the cab empty. Even the driver had bailed.

Fuming, she turned back to Mrs. Halvorsen. Spotting the red-faced, heavyset guy now standing beside her neighbor didn't help Liza's mood. Murph was the ace local reporter for the *Oregon Daily*, the paper where Liza was a columnist. But Murph was a newshound first, a colleague second. As he approached her, pulling out his notebook, he was one hundred percent on the trail of a story.

"How nice to speak to the candidate for a change, instead of some spokesperson," he said with a facetious grin.

"I'm not a . . ." Liza stopped when she saw Murph's pen dancing across the page. "Listen, Murph—off the record," she said. "Can we wait to do this until after I speak with Ava?"

Ava Barnes was Liza's best friend from childhood as well as the managing editor of the *Oregon Daily*. By convincing Liza to create her sudoku column, she'd also become Liza's supervisor . . . as well as Murph's.

"I'm sure the boss would love to chat with you," Murph said. "Especially since she's been working on an editorial endorsing Ray Massini for mayor."

Still giving her that aggravating grin, he nodded, folded up his book, and took off as another familiar figure joined them. Murph was a burly guy, but he seemed downright slender beside the bearlike presence of Sheriff Bert Clements. The sheriff's khakis might look a bit rumpled, but his style was smooth and placid.

"Afternoon, Liza," he said with a nod.

"I hope you don't think this nonsense was my idea." Liza pointed at the float. "Those idiots left this stupid thing blocking traffic."

"Wouldn't want to be seen stifling free speech." Clements's voice sounded mild enough. "Especially when it involves the Party," he continued in an undertone.

A little light began to seep through the darkness of Liza's anger and puzzlement. Elections in Killamook County had been a one-party affair since before she'd been born. And the Party leadership hadn't changed in all that time, either.

"John Jacob Pondscum," Liza growled.

"That's Pauncecombe to you," Clements corrected, pronouncing the name to rhyme with "Rome."

He shook his head. "And I don't think the orders for this little circus came from that high up the food chain. Often, the essence of politics is deniability. This may be a case of the left hand not knowing what the right is doing."

Clements's craggy face creased in a grin. "I suppose I should consider myself lucky you didn't end up running against me."

His smile faded as a new guy in one of those ubiquitous faux straw hats scrambled onto the float and commandeered the mike. Liza took a step toward him until she realized he had a different hatband—the message read, SMUTZ 4 SHERIFF.

"Ladies and gents," the newcomer bellowed into the microphone. "We have some more petitions for you. Sign up, get behind the two brooms that will sweep this town clean. Smutz for sheriff, and Kelly for mayor."

"Who's this clown?" Liza asked in disbelief.

"Oscar Smutz. He was a . . . political appointee on the force until I persuaded him to leave."

"So you've got a corrupt cop running against you for sheriff?" Liza still couldn't quite get her head around all this.

"Not exactly corrupt—just a little too cozy with John Jacob and Company. Whenever they needed to put a badge behind some scheme or other, Oscar was their go-to guy. I'm also afraid he never saw a free lunch that he couldn't eat. Oscar's the kind of guy who'd walk down Main Street and grab himself an apple off the produce stand without paying for it. An opportunist . . ." He nodded toward the float Smutz had taken over. "As you see."

He stepped up to the stalled float. Smutz put his hand over the mike. "Hey, Bert."

"That's 'Sheriff Clements' to you, Oscar," Clements said.

Hands on his hips, Smutz aimed his big beer gut at the sheriff like some sort of weapon. "At least for the time being. I'm gonna change that. And if you got any problems, you can take them up with Mr. Redbourne at the county elections office."

Clements glanced back at Liza. "Free speech and all that." He turned to Smutz again. "But I'm afraid your float is blocking traffic."

"It's not my float," Smutz replied quickly.

"Then maybe you should stop using it." Clements snapped the trap shut fairly gently. "Respect for private property and stuff like that."

As Smutz abandoned his perch, Clements headed up to the truck's open door. Liza looked around for Jimmy Perrine's pickup. It had disappeared, but Liza's luggage stood in a neat pile on the curb.

Guess when he saw I didn't think the joke was too funny, he got out while the getting was good, she thought.

Liza made the rounds of the milling political volunteers until she caught up with Mrs. Halvorsen. "Did you bring your car?" she asked her neighbor.

"I certainly did." Mrs. H. made a clucking noise when she noticed Liza's bags. "Do you need a lift?"

"I certainly do." Liza recalled the exchange between the sheriff and his new political rival, and the glimmer of a plan began to coalesce. "And I think I'd like to borrow your car for a while, if that's okay."

Mrs. H. was only too glad to oblige and had luckily parked her ancient Oldsmobile on the other side of the traffic jam. They managed to load Liza's luggage and get away before Sheriff Clements got the truck started and moved. It was a fairly short drive to Hackleberry Avenue, and offloading the luggage and Mrs. H. didn't take long. Soon Liza set off along a back route to the town of Killamook. She had two destinations. One was the kennel where she'd left her dog, Rusty. The other was the Killamook County Board of Elections.

Driving along Broad Street, Killamook's main drag, was like taking one of those Perfect Americana theme park rides. Every shutter on every house, each sign on every shop, looked like an escapee from the turn of the century—the last century, not the Y2K era. It actually got a little oppressive, especially since Liza knew how highhanded the town's Preservation Council could be.

She hoped she wouldn't encounter the same attitude at the elections office.

The county center was a recent construction and, as

such, had been banished from the business district. It was a brick and concrete slab structure hidden by trees and a tall hedge toward the edge of town. No doubt Party stalwarts had provided all that concrete and landscaping at a healthy markup.

Inside, however, Liza caught a whiff of mildew and noticed telltale stains extending down from the dropped ceilings. She couldn't help recalling one of her mother's favorite lines—an old Japanese saying, or so she claimed: "The bitterness of poor quality remains long after the sweetness of low price has faded."

In Killamook politics, I guess that should be, "The stink of low quality remains long after the high kickbacks get paid off," she thought as she set off in quest of the elections office. Years of practical publicity work had taught her to avoid bureaucratic roadblocks by striding purposefully rather than appearing lost.

She had fewer problems than she'd expected. No heads came up for a glance at the stranger passing by. In fact, the office workers seemed to avoid her eyes, as if strangers meant trouble . . . as if they were afraid.

Off in a dingy corner with an even stronger mildew problem, Liza spotted a door marked C. REDBOURNE. She breezed past and opened it before the secretary even realized she was there.

The heavyset woman stared, her mouth dropping open. "Hey! No one sees Mr. Redbourne without an appointment."

"Well, it's either him or J.J. Pauncecombe." Liza didn't get a chance to say more because she was pulled into the office, the door slamming shut. She was about to make a sharp remark but instead found herself staring.

"Chad?" she gasped in disbelief. "Chad Redbourne?"

You shouldn't be so surprised, that little voice in the back of her head chimed in. *How many Redbournes could there be in Killamook?*

Still, Liza hadn't expected to see the class nerd from her days at Killamook High.

Chad had actually improved over the last twenty years or so. His nose still had an extra inch to it, and so did his chin. His mouth was still too wide, and now his mouse brown hair was getting a little sparse at the hairline. But he'd ditched the Coke-bottle glasses—probably for contacts. And he'd finally grown into that scarecrow frame with the ankles and wrists sticking out of his clothes. He'd also learned to dress, if the suit jacket hanging from the back of the office door was any indication.

"Liza Kelly!" Chad responded in the same tones of disbelief.

"The very same," Liza replied. "How are you doing? The last I heard, you were off to law school." Chad's grandfather was a judge. His career path had probably been determined while he was still in the womb.

"Yeah, well, I passed the bar but didn't do too well in the courtroom." His shoulders jerked in the same hapless gesture Liza remembered from the Killamook High cafeteria.

Come to think of it, a back office functionary's job would make a better fit for the painfully shy Chad.

His head bobbed and he smiled as he walked over to his desk. "I see your name all the time in the newspaper," Chad said. "That's a great column you do on sudoku. Have you ever considered doing a book?"

"Nobody's asked me," Liza told him.

"I've been trying my hand . . ." With a self-deprecating smile, Chad opened a drawer and extracted a sheaf of paper—all half-sheets.

Then Liza realized they were full sheets, folded in half, then meticulously stapled into small booklets. And each page held two familiar-looking boxed arrays—sudoku puzzles. Liza looked at the first.

"You did these?" she asked.

"I find it relaxes me after a long day in the office," Chad said.

"I wish I could say the same—but it's a little different when you're working against a deadline to produce one

	3					7		
					1	8		
7	9				5		6	
			7					5
4			9					3
2			6					
	2		8				1	4
	5	9						
	6					2		

every day." Liza hefted the collection, shaking her head. You never knew where you'd encounter a fan, it seemed. "Still, this is quite an accomplishment. You do have a book here."

She took in Chad's eager expression. "As for getting it published, though, I'm not sure—maybe I could ask a few friends—have you considered doing something on the Internet?"

He shook his head. "Just a thought. To get a real book deal, I expect you'd have to be famous—like you."

"Speaking of which, some people seem to want me even more famous," Liza said, switching conversational gears. "They're popping out of the woodwork with petitions to run me for mayor of Maiden's Bay."

"Ah." Chad's wide lips curled into a bigger—and considerably less genuine—smile. Just one look told Liza he knew all about the "Kelly for Mayor" campaign. "Well, if your friends and neighbors think that highly of you, it must be quite a compliment."

"It might be," Liza said, "if they hadn't waited till my back was turned before they started in."

"Perhaps they wanted to dip a toe in the water before approaching you," Chad suggested.

"Dip a toe?" Liza burst out. "They had a float blocking half the traffic in downtown Maiden's Bay!" She leaned forward across the desk. "What I want to know is how to stop them."

"I'm not sure . . ." Chad gave her a pretty theatrical frown. "I don't know of any electoral rule barring concerned citizens from expressing support for a candidate—or advocating others to support that candidate."

It came out so smoothly, Liza wondered how long Chad had practiced that particular speech. Two weeks, maybe?

"So it's just a question of free speech, is that it?"

Liza's voice oozed sarcasm as she quoted Bert Clements, but Chad pounced on her words gratefully. "That's it exactly. I regret to say there's nothing this office can do."

He carefully replaced his sudoku collection in its drawer, then gestured to the array of papers marshaled across the top of his desk. "It was great to see you again, Liza. Now I'm afraid I have someone coming in for an important meeting . . ."

He ushered her back to the door and opened it. But Liza wasn't about to let him off that easily. She paused in the open doorway. "I suppose you think you've been very nice about this—slick, even. But I think this whole situation stinks as much as the air in here does. Someone's going to swing for it, you can take my word on that."

It was a pretty hollow threat, but the best she could come up with. Liza spun on her heel to make a dramatic exit—and instead collided with Chad's next meeting.

"Hey, I'm always up for swinging," Sergeant Ted Everard told her, catching her by the arm before she landed on her butt and made a complete fool of herself.

"Ted! It's been a while. What brings you back to this part of the state?" Everard worked for the state police, compiling crime-scene statistics. He'd come to Maiden's

Bay to investigate a spike in serious crime there, had gotten involved in a case with Liza—and then gotten involved with Liza in a more personal way.

His long, thin face shut down, going into a version of cop mode. "I'm doing some field work for a state task force."

Then his expression softened a little. "But I hope I'll get the chance to see you again."

Liza nodded, hoping her own face hid the calculations going on inside. At least she was sincere when she said, "I hope so, Ted. And soon."

3

Liza left the county center a lot more slowly than she'd entered, a thoughtful frown on her face. She'd already pushed her next errand—rescuing Rusty from the kennel here in town—to the bottom of her mental list. What she needed now was a nice, cool drink and a shady spot where she could watch the exit from the county center's parking lot without being disturbed.

The first problem was solved with a quick visit back at the business district, where Liza dashed into a coffee shop and emerged with an oversized plastic cup of iced coffee. Judging from the pile of papers on Chad Redbourne's desk, his meeting with Ted wasn't going to be a five-minute deal. She should have ample time to get back before Ted tried to make his escape.

Liza came back to the county center and, just to make sure, toured the parking lot until she spotted the official car that Ted had used on his last visit to town. It was a state police cruiser that had seen better days, being demoted first to an unmarked car and now to mere bureaucratic transportation.

Ted had grown quite profane about his set of government

wheels, not just for the way it ran but also for what it represented. He'd been a damned good investigator until he'd gotten seriously shot up in a bad bust and found himself driving a desk. His accounting degree and facility with numbers had kept him there, massaging crime statistics and occasionally getting out in the field on the trail of some sort of business shenanigans.

That's why Liza wanted to talk with Ted—to find out why he'd come to visit Chad Redbourne.

Driving back to the street, she found a spot under one of the ornamental trees and settled down to wait Ted out.

Liza greedily sucked down the iced coffee—she hadn't realized how parched she'd gotten on the trip up from California to Killamook. It didn't take her long to realize she'd committed one of the classic rookie stakeout mistakes. The caffeine she'd drunk had its usual effect, and by the time Ted finally appeared, Liza feared she was about to disgrace herself.

Her wave as Ted pulled out was considerably more frantic than she'd intended it to be.

Ted stopped his car beside Liza's borrowed Oldsmobile. "Why am I not completely astonished at this turn of events?"

"Maybe it was seeing me at Chad's office," Liza replied.

"So, you want to get a cup of coffee or something?"

Liza repressed a twinge at hearing that, saying, "I'll follow you anywhere—as long as there's a clean bathroom at the end."

"Hmmm . . . sounds like the quicker, the better," Ted replied. He led the way back to Broad Street and a restaurant that just about screamed "Ye Olde Inne."

Liza didn't pay much attention to the décor as she hurried to the ladies' room. She returned to find Ted seated at a table, a steaming bowl in front of him. "Hope you don't mind that I ordered some clam chowder."

"That's what I hate about this place!" Liza burst out.

Ted blinked, a little nonplussed. "The chowder? The table? That they didn't wait for you? The john?"

She shook her head, plumping down into the not-too-comfortable wooden captain's chair. "I just realized where the hell we are. You wouldn't have been around here twenty years ago."

"I guess not, since I grew up in Portland," Ted said.

"Well, when I went to high school, this was Paul's, our favorite burger joint. Everybody went here after classes. Even when the chains moved in, old Paul's was the favorite—they made the best burgers in town."

A pair of creases appeared between Ted's eyebrows. "I don't see—"

"You sure as hell don't see Paul's," Liza cut in. "The Preservation Council decided a lowly burger joint didn't enhance the historical ambience of Broad Street, even though Paul had opened the place more than thirty years ago. So goodbye, great burgers, hello, chowder out of a big can—because the clientele would be tourists who won't know any better."

Everard put down his spoon. "Well, that certainly makes it extra delicious. But I guess I can understand your bitterness."

Liza shook her head. "That's just the start of it." She stabbed a finger toward the front window of the restaurant. "See that boutique with the overpriced outdoor gear across the street? That was a saloon back in the day. My dad would bring me in there for a soda when I was growing up. His picture was on the wall behind the bar—part of a championship softball team from before I was born. Dad looked about seventeen. That place had been part of the community—just about forever. The original owner opened the doors a year before the Depression."

Liza shifted in her uncomfortable chair—designed to keep the tourists from hanging around too long, she figured. "The Preservation Council decided this was no place for a blue-collar bar and banished them to a strip mall outside of town. The joint was gone in a year."

She scowled. "I'm surprised they didn't fob them off on Maiden's Bay instead—although then the bar might have survived."

Ted frowned in puzzlement. "Fob them off?"

"Whatever the powers that be don't want in Killamook, they stick in Maiden's Bay," Liza said. "Killamook gets a Broad Street that never was and the tourist business, Maiden's Bay gets the smelly cannery. Fishing boats berth in Maiden's Bay, but the yacht harbor is down the block over there. I hate to think about it, but my hometown has become the dumping ground of Killamook County. And a lot of it has to do with the people in the county center."

"You mean it has to do with the Killamook machine and John Jacob Pauncecombe," Ted said in a low voice.

Liza leaned across the table. "If you know that name, that suggests you're here after big game."

"Not that big." Ted raised both hands in a cautioning gesture. "I don't know how up you are on all the political ins and outs since you came back to Oregon. But the government has been working to create a statewide voter database for some time now, and the deadline is coming up. I got assigned to the compliance taskforce, following up with counties that can't quite seem to get their acts together."

"Like Killamook and the machine." Liza gave a short, sharp laugh. "God knows how many make-believe voters they've got stocked away."

"It can't be like Chicago in the old days," Ted said. "They used to register whole cemeteries to pad the vote."

"I think Killamook is a little small for that," Liza agreed. "But it's hard to believe that Chad Redbourne is the secret master of all the phony voters."

Ted shrugged. "Well, he's the one in charge of voting—the obvious suspect, you might say. I'll tell you this, though. Our latest meeting was way different from the others over the last couple of weeks. He kept fumbling and bumbling—wasting at least another twenty minutes."

Great—while I sat outside in the car with a bursting bladder, Liza thought.

"At first I thought Redbourne had just come up with a new way to stonewall me. Then I realized he was distracted—no, more than that—scared." Ted gave her a sidelong look. "What the hell were you talking about with him that you left making threats? Because whatever it was, you sure shook him up."

Liza looked down at the tabletop, pursing her lips. She didn't want to be discussing this nonsense, but the words came out anyway. "Some idiots are trying to run me for mayor."

That got a laugh out of Ted. "Madam Mayor—do you think that would outrank a sergeant?"

"Knock it off, Everard," Liza shot back. "It's the last thing I want—or need—right now."

"Makes sense, though, I guess." Ted was back in his more analytical cop mode. "Massini must be gearing up for his own run. Having an unexpected candidate turn up has probably thrown him off his stride. Like it or not, he's got to deal with you. That means diverting assets—people and even money— that might have more usefully been deployed elsewhere."

"Ted, I'm not even for real."

"You know that, Pauncecombe and his people know that, but Massini can't be sure. So, like it or not, he'll have to divert resources—time and brainpower, if not money. And whatever he does, he'll be a little weaker in dealing with the candidate the machine does put up against him. It's a clever example of a political dirty trick—and for Killamook, fairly subtle, as well."

Liza nodded in doubtful appreciation of Ted's analysis. "Well, I went to Chad Redbourne to find out what I could do about it, and got nothing—except a strong suspicion that he's in on whatever is going on. And I still don't know what to do. It's like identity theft, just without all the interesting shopping."

"You could freak them all out and start running for real," Ted suggested.

Liza gave him a look. "Yeah, right."

He shrugged. "Or you could pull a Sherman."

"A what?"

"It's a who, actually, General William Tecumseh Sherman, Civil War hero."

"The guy who said, 'War is hell,'" Liza said.

"He had another interesting quote, more suited to your situation. After the war, a lot of people wanted to put him up for the presidency. He wasn't fond of that prospect, so he told them, 'If nominated, I shall not run; if elected, I will not serve.'"

Liza smiled. "You have to admire the way they had with words in the old days."

Ted nodded. "It worked so well that it became part of the political lingo. If someone wants to reject being drafted for an office, they pull a Sherman."

"I'll have to remember that," Liza said. *Because I guess that's what I'll have to do with Ava for the paper,* she thought.

"At least that clears up your present difficulty, if not your past problems with this place . . ." Ted paused as he realized he'd lost Liza again. "Did you notice another historical annoyance?" he asked.

"Yes," Liza replied, "she's opening the door."

The restaurant's door flew open as a woman in expensive yet garish clothing and makeup popped inside. Curly black hair framed her head like a cloud, and her silk tank top showed off impressive and perfectly tanned cleavage. An abbreviated crimson skirt twitched around her ample hips, and her slim waist was accentuated by a gold belt in the shape of a snake, thousands of tiny scales culminating in a solid gold head with winking ruby eyes.

"Liza Kelly!" the sexy vision purred, giving Liza a vividly lipsticked smile. "I heard you were back in the area . . . I just haven't seen you at the country club."

The only time Liza would turn up at the Killamook Country Club would be as the guest of honor at a funeral—and even then she'd be spinning in her casket.

"Ooh!" Liza's new best friend exclaimed, bringing up a wristwatch that looked like a jewel-encrusted armband. "Got to run—can't keep the hooze-bond waiting. See ya around."

She swung round, her short skirt flicking within a millimeter of decency, and strode off on her four-inch heels.

Ted craned his neck, watching her through the window, then shamefacedly turned back to Liza. "Who was that?"

"I guess you could call her my high school nemesis," Liza replied grimly. "Brandy D'Alessandro."

"D'Alessandro?" Ted echoed. "Isn't that some sort of Italian for 'Alexander'?"

"Tell me about it," Liza snorted. "The cutesy name, the whole Brunette Bombshell thing, skirts up to her crotch, shirts open down to her belly button, captain of the cheer-leading squad . . ."

"Queen Bee," Ted said.

"That's the first letter of five to describe her." Liza closed her eyes, remembering how it was back then. She wasn't bad looking, was pretty popular, and certainly smart. But when Brandy was around, Liza might as well have been wallpaper. "She gave me an itch."

"Guess so, if you still have to scratch it twenty years later."

"We both ran for president of the senior class," Liza said.

"And she won?"

Liza shook her head. "Should have been a sure thing—more girls than guys in the class. Instead, Brandy and I split the vote, and J.J. Pauncecombe—John Junior—got in."

She laughed at the look on Ted's face. "Oh, yeah, he was in our class, too. So was Chad Redbourne. The election wound up a pure popularity poll—with J.J. as president and Brandy as vice president. I was secretary, and Chad was the class treasurer."

Ted sat silent for a moment, then said, "I always think the best thing about high school is that it's so many years ago. You moved on."

Liza nodded. "Back then, I couldn't wait to get away. I made sure the college I chose was as far away as I could manage."

"And then you went to Japan to visit your mom's family, followed by those years down in L.A." Ted spread his hands. "You had a life. Looks like your friend Brandy never got farther than the Killamook Country Club."

"Actually, Brandy headed down to California after high school." Liza smiled. "She thought she was going to set Hollywood on fire. But all she got was a few walk-on parts, basically on the strength of her chest."

Ted shrugged. "From what I could see, she still has a pretty strong chest."

Liza made a rude noise. "That's just because she can afford expensively engineered lingerie to lift and separate whatever she's got under that designer slutwear she struts around in."

"So I guess she must have put away something from the film business."

"No, that was her second career—or actually, her third." Liza gazed out the window for a moment. "Brandy came back to Killamook, and J.J. got her a job in the Party offices. Not surprising—they'd always been an item at school."

"So she married the boss's son?"

Liza couldn't help her malicious smile. "No, but her obvious talents did get some notice from on high. Nowadays, Brandy is Mrs. John Jacob Pauncecombe, Senior—your basic trophy wife."

She managed to time that announcement just as Ted brought his spoon to his lips—and just narrowly avoided getting spattered with clam chowder. Shaking his head, Ted dropped the spoon into his bowl. "What do you say we blow this pop stand?"

"You didn't finish your soup," Liza said.

"And I don't think I'm going to," Ted replied. "You were right. The damned stuff tastes like fish-flavored wallpaper paste."

They had a coffee and bite to eat in a place with fewer past associations for Liza, and then Ted excused himself. "Got to get back to my motel and go over the BS papers Redbourne gave me."

"Business before pleasure, I guess," Liza said.

Ted's lips quirked in a familiar grin. "Maybe you'd change my mind if you paraded around in—what did you call it? Designer slutwear?"

"In your dreams, Everard."

"Ohhhhh, yesssss," Ted replied in a trembling voice, raising his eyes to the sky.

Liza smacked him and went to Mrs. Halvorsen's enormous, Reagan-era Oldsmobile.

"Looks as if I'll be here for a while," Ted called after her. "It will take that much for Redbourne to clear up this particular mess. Will I see you? We'll stay away from the Killamook tourist traps."

"Good plan," Liza told him as she got into the car. "You've got my number."

Ted waved and climbed into his official clunker. Each of them pulled onto Broad Street, heading in opposite directions.

Liza drove to Krista's Killamook Kennels, the only pet-boarding operation in the area. Mrs. H. had volunteered to visit Rusty every day, feeding and walking him. That had been okay for a long weekend, but Liza thought two weeks of doggie duty was pushing the envelope of neighborly friendship.

The only drawback was Krista Cronin's overwhelming sweetness. Liza sometimes wondered if the groomer and kennel owner was a danger to diabetic clients. As soon as she came in the door, Krista began caroling, "Rusty! Rusty! Mommy's here!"

That set off an entire chorus of barks, but the loudest came from Rusty. "Mixed-breed" was far too high-toned a description for the lovable mutt who'd wandered into the neighborhood at the same time that Liza had taken up lonely residence in her old family home.

He'd gotten his name from the color of his coat, suggesting a predominance of Irish setter in his background. As soon as Krista let him out of his cage, he came bounding toward Liza, going into a whole-body wriggle of delight at seeing her. He danced around, barking happily, then leapt up, resting his forepaws on her jean-clad hip.

Liza patted his head. "Good to see you, too, fella. Ready to go home?"

Rusty dropped to the floor with a "Woof!" of assent and trotted for the door.

After a quick exchange with Krista of a check and Rusty's leash, Liza took off after him. She clipped the leash to Rusty's collar, they headed down the block, and he climbed into Mrs. Halvorsen's Oldsmobile, quietly arranging himself on the front seat.

They drove along the coast back to Maiden's Bay with the windows down, Rusty popping his head out every once in a while to catch the breeze, then turning back, apparently to make sure Liza was still there. Liza turned on the radio. "I wonder what kind of taste in music Mrs. H. has."

But instead of music, she got talk. "This is K-MOOK, the Voice of Killamook County," an announcer's voice came out of the speaker.

Liza grimaced. KMUC was the local radio station—not to mention the hobby and personal soapbox of Lawson Wilkes. Wilkes had invested what was supposed to be his college fund into a variety of Silicon Valley enterprises. Some had tanked, but enough had prospered to make him a moderately wealthy man. Unlike a lot of similar investors, he got out of high tech with that small fortune intact. Retiring to the Oregon coast, he'd bought KMUC and adopted the role of mini–media mogul. With a judicious blend of syndicated talk shows, a variety of music, and some local talent, he managed to make a modest profit.

But to establish himself in Killamook, he'd made a deal with a community segment looking for a media outlet—the county's politicians. The community newspaper, more a collection of ads for local stores than a news organ, had collapsed in the nineties. And even before Ava Barnes began running regional operations, the *Oregon Daily* had been hostile to the Killamook machine. Lawson Wilkes and his Owner's Editorials had been a propaganda godsend. WMUC might call itself the Voice of Killamook, but it was really the voice of John Jacob Pauncecombe.

"Now we go to our phone-in forum," the radio host announced. "Do you think that a newcomer to politics—

someone like, say, Liza Kelly, could clean up the mess Ray Massini has made in Maiden's Bay? Let's hear your opinions, people."

Liza stabbed a finger to turn off the radio. But as she drove along, the mood of the day seemed to shift to mirror her own—or rather, Oregon displayed the famous changeability of its weather. The former sunshine quickly dimmed behind a bank of clouds.

Glad I'm safe on the ground heading home instead of up in the air with Wish Dudek, Liza thought, glancing up at the massed gray ranks spreading across the skies. It would be raining soon, and Liza didn't want Rusty celebrating his return home with a vigorous shake in the middle of the living room.

She pulled the Oldsmobile into Mrs. H.'s driveway and left it in front of the garage. Then she opened the door, let Rusty out, and started cutting across the lawn to her own kitchen door.

Dark clouds had gathered to such an extent that the late afternoon seemed more like early evening. And the shadows from the shrubs were deep enough that Liza had no clue as to the identity of the male figure suddenly moving to block her path.

4

Liza recoiled as the tall, dark figure moved toward her. But Rusty bounded forward, his tail wagging a welcome. Since he didn't like most males above the age of ten, this cut down the stalker identity list considerably.

Then the menacing figure stepped into the light and revealed himself as Kevin Shepard.

Liza let out a sigh of relief. Kevin represented a happy memory from high school, as Liza's beau from the football team. She'd returned to Maiden's Bay contemplating divorce and arrived to find Kevin already in Splitsville and starting a new career in the hotel trade, managing the tony Killamook Inn.

A relationship developed, even when Liza's husband, Michael, belatedly turned up hoping for reconciliation. Liza found herself in the middle of a triangle with as much low comedy as romance as Kevin and Michael jostled with each other as jealous suitors. And the whole thing had taken new sides and dimensions when Ted Everard came into Liza's life.

But as Kevin stepped closer, he didn't look all that

affectionate. He seemed more like a man stepping out into enemy, possibly dangerous, territory.

"I heard you were back in town." Kevin's voice was as tight as his facial muscles. "What's going on with the whole mayor thing, Liza? You decide you couldn't live with Massini in charge anymore? Ray's been on the phone to me for days, going nuts."

Oh, that's right. With all the other nonsense going on, Liza had forgotten that she was one of the few who knew Ray Massini's dirty little secret. Like too many attractive and charismatic political animals, Ray thought that every day was mating season. As a single guy home from the Gulf War, he'd cut quite a swath through Killamook County's female population. Unfortunately, he'd kept it up after he married a pillar of local society. And shamefully, Kevin had facilitated, letting his old army buddy carry on trysts at the Killamook Inn.

Discovering Kevin's role in the whole unsavory business had put a severe dent in, not to mention a stain on, his suit of shining armor. Until then, he'd definitely had the edge on Michael when it came to Liza's affections. She sometimes wondered what might have happened if she'd never learned . . .

Right now, though, there were more practical matters to consider. A sex scandal would probably prove fatal to the mayor's bid for a second term. No wonder Massini was going nuts.

"As you said, I was out of town," Liza told Kevin. "I came back to find this nonsense going on—trust me, it's as much a shock for me as it was for you."

"So you're not running?"

"You can tell your friend I'll be pulling a Sherman—I think that's what it's called," Liza said. "I think you'd have to be crazy to get involved in the kind of politics they play around here."

She shook her head. "As far as I'm concerned, exposing Massini's character flaw wouldn't just kill his mayoral campaign. It would also kill the good he's trying to do for Maiden's Bay—the reforms he's trying to make. Then J.J. Pauncecombe and his cronies win."

A chilling thought struck her—and she saw it reflected on Kevin's face.

"Do you think the other side knows about the mayor's little adventures?" Liza asked.

Kevin's features relaxed a little. "I'm glad to hear you think we're on the same side. As for your question . . ." He shrugged. "I don't think so, or we'd have heard it on KMUC by now."

"Guess so." Liza frowned. Michelle might not dabble in politics, but the Markson Agency kept professional tabs on how competitors did their jobs. "The boys in Killamook don't seem to be too subtle. With other political operations, I might expect a whispering campaign to start off with. You haven't heard anything?"

Kevin shook his head. "From a professional standpoint, would you say that's good?"

Now it was Liza's turn to shrug. "If they had a bomb like that to drop, they could take Massini out in a single news cycle. Why would they piddle around with this foolish fake campaign for me?"

As if on cue, Rusty suddenly headed into the bushes.

"Speaking of piddling," Liza said with a wry smile.

Kevin's smile showed more relief than humor. "So I can definitely tell Ray you're out of the race." He paused for a second. "And that the other thing seems okay."

"It doesn't seem to be public knowledge," Liza corrected. "I don't think it's okay."

Kevin's face shut down—he obviously didn't know how to answer that. "I don't know what's going on with that anymore." He directed his gruff voice to the ground. "I never wanted to."

"I think that's just as well," Liza said.

He raised his eyes. "So we're good?"

She nodded.

"Good." Kevin started down Liza's driveway just as thick, heavy raindrops began to fall.

Liza gave Rusty's leash a tug. "I hope you have no surprises for me."

They came in through the kitchen door, so Rusty could shake himself dry on the linoleum floor. Not for the first time, Liza wished she could do the same.

It's amazing how freaking wet you can get covering just fifteen feet, she thought, trying to pull her sodden T-shirt away from her skin.

The phone rang, and Liza spun to give it an uneasy glance. Sometimes Michael seemed to display an almost paranormal awareness of when she was with Kevin—he seemed to call just as his rival left or hung up.

Looking at the caller ID screen, Liza let her breath hiss out from between her teeth. "Not Michael—Michelle," she muttered. "This could get even worse."

She picked up the receiver, to hear her partner begin without preamble, "As you start your career in public service, I hope you'll recall that this agency does not do political campaigns."

Forget about Michael's ESP, Michelle's information-gathering antennas rivaled the NSA's—especially when it came to using celebrity. Liza's quota of fame might just barely get her mentioned on a small-market radio station but Michelle had obviously heard about it.

"I wish I could say it was a hoax," Liza said. She could just imagine her partner on the other end of the connection, probably perched on the front of her desk, her delicate, almost elfin, features set somewhere between a frown and a pout.

People sometimes described Michelle Markson as the fairy princess of Bad Attitude. They just never said that to her face, because Michelle didn't need a magic wand to wreak havoc on people's lives and careers. She used the power of the pen and a caustic tongue to shear huge chunks of ego and self-esteem off some of Hollywood's biggest shots, carving out an impressive turf for herself as a leading warlord of publicity.

Michelle didn't pull her punches, even with friends. "So you're taking another leave of absence from the agency—and your senses? It's bad enough you apparently go underground for weeks, but then I start getting these outré reports—"

"I took some time off to recharge my batteries," Liza said. "I don't think I have to defend that to someone who famously goes absolutely incommunicado from the office."

"I might do that for a relaxing weekend," Michelle replied, "and besides, I have a staff to deal with any messes that might crop up."

Intimating that whatever Liza might be doing, she was creating a mess. "You still haven't explained this sudden plunge into politics."

"I haven't plunged." Liza tried to keep the edge out of her voice. "Somebody dunked me."

As she explained the progress of her invented candidacy, Michelle became ominously silent. "As I said, the agency doesn't do political campaigns. But this travesty affects your image—our image—*my* image. I wouldn't be averse to taking a little constructive action against whoever is responsible."

Knowing Michelle, the operative word would be more "destructive" than "constructive."

"Better, I think, for me just to extricate myself and let this whole situation die a natural death," Liza said.

"In that case, you shouldn't be talking to me, you should be talking to the media," Michelle told her. "Maybe your newspaper friend can be of some help."

Her dismissive tone was directed partly at Liza, and partly at mere print media. "Better get started right away. It only becomes harder to get rid of rumors when they've been lying around for a while."

Liza had to bite her lip at that. Considering that she knew about the whole situation only a few hours longer than Michelle, being accused of dawdling felt grossly unfair.

"Thanks for the advice," she finally said. "I'll get on to Ava directly."

"Excellent." Brusque as ever, Michelle cut the connection.

As she hung up, Liza's finger went to the speed-dial button coded with Ava's office number. Then she shook her head. Before spiking the story on this con-job candidacy, there was someone else she had to speak with. Heading around to the front door, she rooted out an umbrella and went next door to break the news to Mrs. Halvorsen.

Actually, the visit with her neighbor had some benefit when Liza finally spoke with Ava sometime later. It allowed her to organize her thoughts beyond a bald withdrawal of her name from consideration.

"About this whole running for mayor thing," she told Ava when she got her on the phone, "I'm issuing a definite Sherman. If nominated, I won't run—"

"I think that's 'shall not,'" her editor corrected.

"Fine, you can look up the classic line and use that," Liza replied. "I won't run and I won't serve." She paused for a second. "For the people who were out with the petitions—and Mrs. H. assures me that a lot of them were genuine volunteers—I need to say thanks very much. I found it very flattering that they thought I could do some good for the town."

"Good for the town," Ava muttered, obviously scribbling down Liza's comments. "You don't want to make any endorsements?"

"I'll leave that to you on the editorial page," Liza told her. "Just say that I'm sure they can find someone more qualified."

"And that's it?" Ava's voice sounded a little clipped.

"From the way Murph was talking, I thought you'd be relieved."

"Maybe Murph thought he'd lose his shot at an exclusive if he mentioned how aggravated I was," Ava told her. "You disappear without a word, this whole 'Liza for Mayor' thing starts up—if it weren't for the fact that you'd added so many columns to your cushion, I might have thought you'd been kidnapped."

"Thanks—I think," Liza replied. "I just knew that extra work would pay off."

"By the way, we only have a few pieces left in the can," Ava said in impeccable managing editor mode. "I hope you spent part of your vacation writing."

"Ah." Liza sighed. Back to the old rat race.

"And you might have told me you were going." Now Liza's childhood friend was peeking out from under the editor's mantle.

"Maybe I should have," Liza admitted, "but my last few announced trips didn't turn out that well. People ended up dead. I just wanted to get away . . . on my own. I didn't even go as Liza Kelly, I went as Mrs. Michael Langley."

"Wow—really undercover," Ava said facetiously. "And then you got one hell of a welcome home."

"Let's just say I may not be responsible if I meet a guy named Clark Hagen. Mrs. H. told me he's the one who did the dirty work, recruiting her and the other volunteers."

"Well, he's not one of the big gears in the Pauncecombe machine," Ava said.

"What about Chad Redbourne?"

"He's come onto our radar, and not just for alumni reunions."

"I saw him today," Liza said, "for the first time since the summer after senior year."

"He cleaned up pretty well, all things considered. Still unmarried after all these years. I thought of going out with him for a while after my divorce." Ava sounded a little embarrassed to admit that.

Liza laughed. "I think you were right to take a pass on that. He still had that whole fumbly nervous thing going when I talked with him." She paused for a second. "In fact, everybody at the county center seemed a bit on edge—as if they were afraid the ax was going to come out. Is the fiscal crisis that bad?"

"I've noticed that myself, talking to people in the government," Ava said. "I guess people are taking their cue from the top. Old Man Pauncecombe—well, he *is* an old man these days, and his temper has gotten kind of . . . erratic. If he hears something he doesn't want to hear, he flies off the handle."

"How far?" Liza asked.

"The last big blowup I heard about happened after the paper shone a little light on John Junior trying to finagle the school's milk contract. I mean, that was really low."

"And you've got a kid going there," Liza added.

"Anyway, there was such a stink, J.J. had to let his little deal die. And when he had to report that there wouldn't be any kickbacks, John Jacob chased him out of the house with a twelve-iron."

Huh, Liza thought. *With a husband like that, I don't think Brandy D'Alessandro landed herself in a bed of roses.*

Aloud, she said, "Getting into that whole 'shoot the messenger' thing isn't the smartest idea. You don't get much in the way of honest information."

"I hope that's not a comment on my management style," Ava told her.

"No, but it just may be the Achilles' heel of the Killamook machine," Liza said. "Everybody at the county offices was tiptoeing around, but Ted Everard said Chad was especially bad during their meeting."

"So you bumped into Ted Everard, did you?" Ava's voice became determinedly nonchalant. "He's been in town several times on this task force thing. Stopped by our office asking if I knew where you might be."

"I met him at Chad's office, and we got together afterward. The thing is, Ted asked what I'd said to Chad to get him so shook up. Oh, I tried to rake Chad over the coals for this petition thing, but I really had nothing."

"So?" Ava asked.

"I don't think it was anything Chad heard," Liza said slowly. "I think it was what he saw—that Ted and I are pretty tight. Whoever hatched this whole 'Kelly for Mayor' scheme didn't do their homework. But Chad saw that the guy who's looking into voter record problems is personally connected with someone being harassed through their electoral shenanigans."

"Namely, you." Ava sounded doubtful. "From what I know of Ted Everard, his feelings won't affect his investigation."

"But from Chad's point of view, Ted has all the more incentive to root out any ghost voters. If that happens, he's afraid that the higher-ups in the machine will just leave him out to dry—or worse, if John Jacob gets angry enough. He's afraid that he'll be blamed for a disaster that someone else created."

"You sound as if you're going someplace with this," Ava said, "but I'm not sure where."

"I'm going to Chad Redbourne's place," Liza told her. "Can you give me the address?"

"I've got it in the Rolodex," Ava replied. "But what do you expect to do there?"

"I may not be able to fight for truth, justice, and the American way," Liza said. "But with luck, I might shake the name behind this one dirty trick out of him."

"And then?"

"Then I can put their head on a stick in my front yard next to the mailbox."

That flippant reply just made Ava more dubious, but in the end she gave Liza the address she wanted—after extracting a promise of more columns ASAP. On that agreement, they hung up.

Liza still sat in her improvised living room office space, regarding the Killamook address she'd written down with satisfaction. Then Rusty came over, nudged her knee, and real life intruded on her revenge fantasies. A quick tour of the kitchen revealed that she was out of dog food—and the people-food situation wasn't that much better. Liza had made a concerted effort to use up all the perishables before leaving on vacation. She didn't want to come home to find some gray or green muck growing on something she'd left in the refrigerator.

"Shopping," she said. "And I'm still carless until I get up to Portland. Looks like a case of going back to Mrs. H. again."

By the time she'd gotten Mrs. Halvorsen's Oldsmobile, done her shopping, and fed Rusty, it was early evening. The rain had stopped, replaced with a watery overcast that shadowed the setting sun.

"Looks later than I think," Liza muttered as she drove along the coast of the bay.

She turned off onto side roads, making her way into what her mother would have called an upper-middle neighborhood. The homes were still modest enough, but the building lots were bigger, with plenty of shrubbery to ensure privacy.

Pulling up at the address, Liza realized she'd been here a couple of times for some excruciating high school parties—the kind where parents forced the supposed host into inviting people over and only good manners forced the invitees to respond. None of the cool kids came, in spite of the pool, the extensive barbecue, or the expensive sound system in Chad's backyard.

A scrap of gossip floated up from her memory—Mom mentioning that the Redbournes had retired to Arizona in search of a sunnier lifestyle.

So I guess Chad is alone in there, Liza thought.

She parked at the end of the drive and walked up to the front door. Nobody answered when she rang the bell, but she could hear music—The Clash, if she wasn't mistaken— blaring from those famous outdoor speakers.

Maybe he's in the backyard and doesn't hear the bell. Liza moved round to the garden gate and opened it. "Hey, Chad?" she called. "You out here?"

She stepped onto the stone terrace that had been quite the big thing back in the day, sniffing for any trace of barbecue. No smells, no Chad.

Could he have recognized my voice and decided to hide? Liza sighed. That would be classic Nerdbourne behavior.

Well, I didn't hear any doors slamming. So if he's

hiding, he's out here, Liza thought. *And that leaves . . . the Grotto.*

If the terrace brought the Redbournes into the local landscaping avant-garde, their architectural folly pushed them way over the top. They'd actually built a combination arbor and cave, a beehive-shaped, ivy-covered structure in a wooded corner of their property. Nowadays Liza could smile at the pretension. Back in high school, unkind souls had sniggered that the best make-out spot in town belonged to the kid least likely to use it.

Liza headed over in that direction, expecting to catch a few branches in the face. But apparently there was still a path of sorts, the undergrowth trimmed back.

"Chad," she called, "come on out. No sense in making this ridiculous."

She stepped to the mouth of the artfully rough stone structure, peering into the dimness inside. Yes, it was still nice, dark, and private, perfect make-out territory. And it hadn't been abandoned. The cushions on the rustic wooden bench in the back looked new.

Will I have to poke around under there to root him out? Liza thought in exasperation.

She rolled her eyes . . . and that's when she noticed the feet dangling just above her head.

Liza lurched into reverse with a squawk—and rammed into something soft but unyielding behind her.

A hand landed on her shoulder, and she realized it was *someone*, not something. Without even thinking, Liza thrust back with her elbow, catching the owner of the hand in the solar plexus.

He let out with a squawk even louder than the one she'd made. Then, gasping, he stumbled back . . . and tumbled over a wheelbarrow Liza hadn't even noticed.

She'd already whirled to confront . . . a stranger. No, he looked vaguely familiar, but she couldn't quite place the bald head, the doughy face—

The stranger scrambled up from the undignified heap he'd made, trying to keep one eye on Liza while his gaze kept being drawn to the dangling form in the folly.

Liza's one glance had told her that was Chad Redbourne suspended up there. That had been enough for her.

She lashed out with her foot, sweeping the guy's foot out from under him. He crashed into the wheelbarrow again, yelling, "What are you doing?"

"You're not getting out of here." Liza's voice came out

a lot more hoarsely than she'd intended, as if she were breathing hard through a tight throat.

The man's hand darted under his suit jacket, and Liza stopped breathing altogether.

This is where I get shot.

The thought galvanized her into action. She just about tore the cell phone from the pocket of her jeans, shouting, "I'm calling 911!"

The man's hand came into view also clutching a phone. "No, *I* am!"

Sheriff Clements shook his head, looking from Liza to the pair of feet still gently swaying in the entrance of the bee-hive structure. "Maybe I should just give you my office number to put on speed dial, and we can eliminate the middleman."

"I—I didn't expect to find . . . that." Liza jerked her head in the direction of Chad's hanging body, squeezing her eyes shut.

That didn't erase the image that seemed engraved behind her eyeballs—an image she feared she'd see in a lot of night-mares to come. Chad drooped above her like a marionette with all but one string cut. But that string—or rather, rope—had looped around his neck, leaving his face congested and contorted. From the looks of it, Chad's last moments hadn't been pleasant. His too-wide mouth stood open and twisted, as if he'd either been struggling to draw in breath—or had pushed it all out in a final, now-silent scream.

While Liza tried to shake that away, her playmate from ring-around-the-wheelbarrow stepped forward. "Sheriff, I want that woman arrested. I came in here to find her stand-ing in front of a dead body, and then she attacked me."

Clements looked at him. "And you are?"

The stranger fished a card out of his wallet and handed it over.

"Clark Hagen, political consultant," Clements read aloud. "Well, Clark, what were you doing here?"

"Mr. Redbourne called me this afternoon, asking me to stop by this evening. When I arrived, I couldn't get an answer at the door. So I followed the music to the back. I caught a glimpse of color in the trees"—he gestured to Liza's T-shirt—"and I found poor Chad hanging there and this woman stepping back. I put a hand on her shoulder—"

"If you did that after she just found a body, knocking you ass over teakettle might not exactly be an overreaction," Clements interrupted. He turned to Liza. "What do you have to say?"

"I didn't know who was behind me," Liza replied. "For all I knew, it could have been the person who'd just strung up poor Chad.

"Of course, if I'd only known it was Clark here . . ." She shot him a dirty look. "I'd have swung harder."

Turning from a dumbfounded Clements, Liza stuck out a hand to Hagen. Automatically, he began shaking with her. "We didn't get a chance to meet earlier today. I think you left after you heard my name being shouted. I'm Liza Kelly."

The political consultant released her hand as if it had gone red-hot.

Liza turned back to the sheriff. "This is the political genius who left the float blocking the traffic circle in the middle of town."

"The one I had to move?" Clements asked in a deceptively mild voice.

"Yep. Clark went to all that effort, just to get me elected mayor—or so Mrs. Halvorsen tells me."

"Is that so?" Clements showed even more interest. "I find it kind of funny that you couldn't recognize your own client."

Hagen hunched his shoulders a little and fiddled with the knot of his tie. "I was approached to jump-start a grassroots petition campaign in a very restricted time frame," he admitted.

"Didn't you think it kind of strange that the

candidate—which is to say, me—wasn't around to campaign?"

Hagen gave a stiff shrug. "I've seen these things arranged to convince a dubious candidate that a run would be feasible."

"But it could also be arranged as a political dirty trick—creating a straw man or woman to distract the opposition," Liza pointed out. "I wonder, given your obvious range of experience, which happens more often—a campaign as clincher or a campaign as a sham?"

Hagen had no answer for that.

"I'm even more interested in finding out who wanted me to become mayor—even though I didn't want to be," Liza went on. "Who hired you, Clark? Who was your local contact?"

Hagen tugged so vigorously on his tie knot that Liza feared he'd end up like Chad. "I'm not altogether sure," the political operative said. "I was contacted via e-mail, but there was no name on the account. When I arrived in town, there was an envelope waiting for me at the motel desk, containing expense money."

"Must have been a pretty thick envelope, if you were able to pull that float together." Clements shook his head. "And all for someone you didn't know—for a client you didn't know, either. Why would you do that?"

Clark Hagen shrugged his shoulders. "As you said, Sheriff, it was a pretty thick envelope."

That was that. Liza didn't get any of her questions answered. But Sheriff Clements made sure he got in-depth answers for all of his. He had a police cruiser accompany Liza while she returned the Oldsmobile to Mrs. H. and then give her a lift to the police station in downtown Maiden's Bay.

"I thought this would be a little more convenient for you," Clements said. "Hagen went to headquarters in Killamook to talk with Brenna Ross."

Separate the witnesses, Liza thought. *I guess that's standard operating procedure even for a suicide.*

Clements didn't bring out the rubber hose, but he was certainly thorough. Even after Liza gave a nearly step-by-step recital of her visit to Chad's house, her grisly discovery, and her tussle with Clark Hagen, the sheriff wasn't satisfied. He went over her whole afternoon from the moment she'd parted company with him downtown to his arrival in response to her 911 call.

He's just doing his job, Liza told herself as she tried her best to be a good citizen and answer fully.

Then, looking over his notes, Clements said, "So, you knew the deceased before you visited him at the county center?"

That was sufficiently out of left field that Liza hesitated for a moment. Clements looked up from his scribbling like the cartoon image of a good old bear, saying nothing.

Liza had seen Michelle Markson use the technique—hell, she'd done it herself. Let the silence stretch out until the other person in the room—client, interviewee, interrogation subject—would say almost anything to fill the void.

"I knew him way previously," Liza finally said. "We went to high school together. It had to be about twenty years since I'd seen him."

"But you'd been to his house back then?" Clements asked.

"A few times," she admitted. "Chad wasn't exactly the most popular guy in school. I think more people went over there uninvited . . ."

She broke off as a memory crept up from the back of her brain.

"Uninvited?" the sheriff prompted.

"For practical jokes," Liza finished. "Chad was always the guy who'd find his notebook marinated in Coke—or worse, who'd have the spark plugs or even the tires disappear off his car, who'd answer the front door and find the flaming bag of dog crap . . ."

"Something else made you stop," Clements said.

Liza nodded. "One Halloween, somebody strung up a

dummy in the Grotto—that's what they called that old bee-hive thing. Mrs. Redbourne—Chad's mother—nearly had a stroke when she stumbled across it."

She looked down at the scarred tabletop. "I wonder if that's what gave Chad the idea."

Clements shifted in his seat. "You seem to be taking this very personally."

Liza looked him in the eye. "You mean, with all the stiffs I keep stumbling over, I should be getting more blasé about it?"

She took a deep breath. "I hollered at him, and I went over there because I hoped I could shake some information out of him—find out who was behind this BS 'Kelly for Mayor' thing. And I'm the one who found him hanging up there. When it comes to why, though, I think you're more plugged into the politics of this county than I am. You'd have a better idea as to why Chad might have been in trouble than I would."

That pretty much ended the discussion. Liza declined the offer of a lift home from another police car.

She stepped out of the town hall to find that full darkness had fallen. Ordinarily, a stroll up to Hackleberry Avenue on a summer evening should have been fairly pleasant. But by the time she'd left the business district behind, Liza realized she'd made a tactical error accepting a cup of the sheriff's awful coffee.

Still worse was the realization that Rusty was probably also suffering from the same symptoms of bursting bladder.

Liza picked up the pace, virtually sprinting for the kitchen door and then the solace of the bathroom. She emerged to find Rusty waiting for her, his leash in his mouth.

"I know exactly how you feel," she told him, clipping the lead to his collar.

They headed straight for the bushes and then took a more leisurely stroll up and down the block. As she let Rusty examine any calling cards his canine colleagues might have left, Liza let her mind go comfortably blank, living in the moment like her dog. She'd gotten pretty aggravated with the sheriff toward the end of their interview. Where did that come from?

Feeling a bit more composed, Liza led Rusty back to the house. They'd almost reached the driveway when she spotted a pair of headlights turning onto Hackleberry Avenue. The quiet residential street didn't get much traffic after folks came home from work, so Liza was a little surprised as the car coasted up to her. Okay, maybe a bit worried but also surprised.

Then she recognized the car as Ted Everard's official clunker—and Ted's long, lean face behind the driver's wheel.

He opened the car door. "I tried to call but got your machine and then your cell voice mail."

Rusty edged closer to the car, his nose up and sniffing. Then he burst out in delighted barking as Ted emerged with a bucket of chicken.

"I figured you might not have eaten." Ted leaned back inside and came out with a six-pack of beer, condensation gleaming on the bottles.

"I knew there was a reason I keep letting you come around," Liza said, leading the way to the door.

They established themselves in the kitchen with plates of chicken and sides. Rusty happily lay under the table, working on one of the chicken thighs, deboned and denuded of breading.

"Well, this makes a change from spa cuisine." Liza took a swig of beer from her bottle. "That was good timing on your part—I was just beginning to think about something to eat."

"I wish I could take credit for that." Ted grimaced. "But I got the heads-up from Bert Clements—after he asked me about bumping into you at Chad Redbourne's office this afternoon."

Liza's bottle hit the tabletop with a bang. "You mean he actually came after you to check up on my story as if I were a—a—"

"Suspect?" Everard finished for her. Liza noticed that he tried to keep his voice very gentle as he used the word.

It didn't help much.

"Yeah!" Liza replied, her mellow mood going up in smoke from a flare of annoyance. "You would think he knows me well enough—"

"It's not about knowing—or trusting," Ted told her. "Anytime anyone, um, translates to the astral plane . . ." He made a floating gesture with his hand, looking up to heaven—or in this case, the kitchen ceiling. "Without either a fatal illness or a physician in attendance, it has to be treated as a suspicious death."

"So Clements is suspicious—of me?" Liza demanded.

"No, but he's covering all the procedural bases." Ted hesitated for a moment, but finally went on. "When you turned up that dead guy in your bed, we did the same—and quickly found out that at the estimated time of death, you were in the dining room of the Killamook Inn, with several witnesses to vouch for you."

Liza fixed him with a gimlet eye. "And did Clements do that, or you? I seem to recall that our first meeting didn't go all that well."

Ted did his best to look angelic. "I'll always remember what you were wearing."

"That's because all I was wearing was a towel—and not much of one, at that," Liza snarled. "I want an answer, Ted. Was it Clements checking me out, or you?"

"Maybe you'd better define 'checking out,' " Ted began, but quickly raised his hands in a placating gesture when Liza brought back her fist. "Calm down. I heard how you decked the other witness on the scene."

He looked at her across the table. "For your information, what annoyed me when I met you was the damned 'amateur sleuth' thing. I thought it would complicate the whole investigation."

"You wouldn't have solved it without me," Liza told him.

Ted shrugged, not arguing the point. "You have to admit, it was a pretty weird case. And right at the beginning, I made it a point to verify your alibi. Thought maybe you and the local sheriff were too friendly. But I found that Clements had been on the job before me—thoroughly."

Before Liza could come up with a reply, the phone rang. "Why do I have to keep reminding you that you work for a newspaper—at least part-time?" an aggravated Ava Barnes demanded without even a "hello."

"I—uh—" Liza said.

"When you see news, you're supposed to contact the newspaper," Ava went on.

"Sorry, I still don't think 'newspaper' when I see dead bodies," Liza finally replied. "At least this time around, it was a suicide."

"Thank God for that," Ava sighed, calming down a little. "This election cycle will be messed up enough without a murder mucking up the works. So I'm going to put Murph on. What can you tell him?"

It was bad enough doing a verbal dance with Ava's ace reporter, but Liza had to do it under the eyes of a cop—a friendly cop, but a cop nonetheless.

She managed to get through it all without ticking off either Murph or Ted. Letting out a long breath, Liza hung up and leaned back against the back of the couch.

Ted handed her a chicken leg. "Y'know, you handled that whole interview thing really well," he said. "Maybe you should consider it as a regular line of work."

Liza waved the chicken leg like a miniature mace. "Done that—but I think I like this sudoku gig of mine better."

They finished their chicken in silence, but it was a friendly silence.

Liza offered Ted another bottle of beer, but he shook his head. "I've got a night of work ahead, and then an early morning. Still got to go through all the nonsense papers Redbourne gave me today so I can brace whoever replaces him tomorrow."

Liza got to her feet as well. "You know, we've all been over the how and the when of this whole thing, but nobody wants to talk about the why."

Her voice wobbled a little on the last word, and Ted stepped forward to take her in his arms. "This has nothing to do with you, and everything to do with the way they play politics in this county," he told her.

"You said he was so scared after he saw me—or us," Liza said into his chest.

"I think he's been scared for a long time, and it just showed," Ted said. "After that chowder we almost had, I stopped by your newspaper to browse through the morgue. I wanted to see how past political scandals went down, maybe find some leverage I could put on Redbourne. I'll tell you this, Liza, the Killamook machine is very big on the rotten apple theory. As soon as somebody gets caught with his hand in the cookie jar, the others close ranks and throw him to the wolves. That's how Bert Clements got to become sheriff, you know. The former incumbent fell foul of a sting operation, so Pauncecombe and the boys dumped him and had to let an obviously honest man get in."

"And Chad?" Liza asked.

Ted sighed. "I think your pal Chad pretty much found himself facing an impossible set of choices. He was sure to face prison time over falsified records in his department, and if he tried to do a deal, he'd become an unperson in Killamook. His life here would be over."

"So he ended it?"

"I think," Ted replied, "that he decided to hang himself rather than let those other bastards leave him dangling in the wind."

He rose and gave her a kiss flavored with seven secret herbs and spices. "Be sad for your friend. But be glad you're out of it, Liza."

6

Liza decided to take Ted's advice. So, after a quick cleanup of chicken buckets and beer bottles, she went to bed.

Her bedroom didn't boast a pillow-top mattress or some other sort of sleep engineering, but it was familiar—and it was home. She slept well—no hanging body nightmares— and woke refreshed. After a quick shower, she threw on a pair of cutoffs and a sloppy top. Then she went downstairs to the kitchen to feed herself and Rusty.

After breakfast, she took the dog out for his morning constitutional. And then, finally, she sat down in front of her computer. Vacation was now officially over. Time to start working up a new reserve of daily articles for the *Oregon Daily* and the other papers syndicating her column.

Let's try to warm up the old sudoku muscles with a fairly easy puzzle, she thought.

But Liza didn't get very far before the phone rang.

She glanced at the bleating instrument. *Let the answering machine take it.*

But then Mrs. Halvorsen's voice came out of the box. "Liza, dear, are you there? I saw you out walking with Rusty before . . ."

It took a moment for Liza to shift mental gears and rise to get the handset. "Hey, Mrs. H. What's up?"

"It may upset you, but I think you'd better turn on the radio."

"Which station?"

"KMUC."

Liza put the phone aside, went into the kitchen, turned on the radio, and tuned in the local station.

"Whoop! Whoop! Whoop!" a loud voice came out of the speaker.

"And welcome back to Drivetime with the Killamook Krew!" a second more nasal voice announced.

Liza blinked in surprise. The station's drivetime show specialized in a little music, some traffic, brief newscasts, and a lot of rude, crude "humor."

Liza picked up the kitchen extension. "You listen to this?" She had to raise her voice over more mouth noises from the radio. "Ah-oooo-gah!"

"It's the only station that comes in on my kitchen set," Mrs. H. replied.

Liza made a mental note to get her neighbor a new radio.

"What did you . . ." Liza broke off as a brief snippet of patriotic fife and drum music came out of the radio.

"Election Update!" the nasal voice intoned.

The goofier, mouth-sound-effects voice came in, trying to sound like one of the pundits from a Sunday morning political show. "September's primary may be in serious trouble because of the death of the county elections commissioner. Indications are that the results will be disputed and end up in a higher court."

"Where are you getting that, Neal?" Nasal Voice asked.

Neal went back into his silly voice. "It's what happened the last time we had Hanging Chad."

Liza winced. Almost as soon as she'd encountered the tragic scene in the Redbournes' Grotto folly, the irreverent electoral reference had popped into her mind.

She figured Ava and the *Oregon Daily* would have too much class to stoop that low. But of course, it was right up the Killamook Krew's alley.

"Y'know, Hanging Chad was found by our own local Miss Marple—Liza Kelly," the nasal-voiced member of the duo said. "She's cracked a lot of cases round these parts and down in California, too."

"I've seen her picture in the paper, Jeff," Loudmouth chimed in, breathing heavily. "She can crack my case anytime she likes. Ah-ooooh-gah!"

"I just hope she can explain why Chad Redbourne cracked up like that," Nasal Jeff went on.

"I heard them mentioning your name," Mrs. Halvorsen's voice came over the telephone, "and I thought you should know. Maybe you could do something about it—call up the radio station, perhaps."

Right—that's just what good old Neal and Jeff would love, so I could be the butt of their half-assed wit, Liza thought.

"They're invading your privacy," Mrs. H. pressed on. "Every day it seems I'm hearing people complain about that on the TV."

"It wouldn't help," Liza explained to her older friend. "That moron on the radio mentioned seeing my picture in the newspaper. They'd argue that makes me a public figure—and fair game for their so-called humor."

"It's not right," Mrs. H. muttered angrily.

"But something we just have to live with," Liza told her. "If it annoys you that much, I suggest you turn off the radio. That's what I'm going to do."

Her neighbor sighed. "If you say so, dear." Then she hung up.

Liza did the same and then followed her own advice, turning off the radio. Not that she was as calm as she'd tried to sound for Mrs. H. What she'd really like to do was throw the damned radio out the window. Or even better, *through* the window . . .

Maybe she was beginning to see the Killamook machine

under every bed, but that childish skit seemed to come right out of their political playbook: close ranks and dismiss Chad Redbourne as a bad apple. A *crazy* bad apple. That was easy enough to do, since he wasn't around to challenge their insinuations.

Just like I wasn't around when they started running me for mayor, Liza suddenly thought.

That realization was enough to send her stomping back to the living room. But before she could burn off her feelings in a burst of creative sudoku energy, she had to hang up the phone she'd left off the hook there.

As soon as she got the handset back in the cradle, the damned thing started ringing again.

The idea of letting the machine pick up was really tempting—but look what happened the last time she'd tried that.

Sighing, Liza brought the phone to her ear. "Hello?"

"I just wanted to call and see how you're doing."

The pleasure Liza felt at hearing her semidivorced husband's voice fizzled as she listened to his tone—concerned, but trying to hide it with casualness.

"So what did you hear that made you call?" she asked Michael a bit more sharply than she meant to.

"You were on the morning news—they said you'd found another body—"

"God*damn* it!" Liza burst out. "You'd think with all the other things going on in the world, news organizations would have something better to talk about."

"Like it or not, you're getting kind of famous," Michael said.

"Right. And the news isn't really news unless there's a celebrity involved. Let Joe Shmoe go out in his fishing boat and overturn it, and it's a two-day local story at best. Put two pro football players in the same boat, and it's in the national news cycle for a week." Liza realized she was gripping the handset so tightly, her finger hurt. "I was in New York a while ago, and I heard a story about a fire at a stable. The hook was all about how hard it was to get the panicked horses out. More recently, I was there when a story about an explosion at a posh kennel aired. Same news-people, same sort of story, so what was the hook? A lot of show dogs died, but the big news was that Martha Stewart lost a puppy being boarded there."

"I'm sure she was genuinely upset," Michael said.

"Of course! Think how I'd feel if something happened to Rusty!"

Hearing his name, Rusty twined his way around Liza's legs and barked.

"Well, yes, that would be terrible." A bit of the sympathy leaked away from Michael's voice, but then, he was allergic to dogs.

"It's as though things aren't really real unless people see them through the lens of celebrity. That can't be good."

"No, it can't." Michael paused for a second, then added, "That's why I thought I should get the real story from you."

"It was a suicide," Liza told him. "Didn't the news report say that?"

"They called it an *apparent* suicide. And with your track record . . ." Michael let that thought die away into silence.

Liza quickly filled him in on the political skullduggery, her run-in with Chad, and her later grisly discovery. "I think he'd gotten himself boxed into an impossible position. When I went to his office, I bumped into Ted Everard—"

"What was he doing there?" Michael interrupted, his voice going a bit flat at the mention of a romantic rival.

"Interrogating Chad, I think, trying to get the lowdown on the voter lists Chad controlled. If the government gets this statewide voter database established—well, it's not a case of *if* but *when*—a whole lot of phony voters are going to show up. There's no getting out of it, and I guess Chad saw himself being set up as the scapegoat."

"So he killed himself?" Michael asked in disbelief.

"You didn't know Chad," Liza said. "He wasn't the toughest guy in the world. Maybe he thought it was better than suffering a long, drawn-out public trial with all his former colleagues vilifying him."

"Well, however it happened, it can't have been enjoyable for you, finding him hanging." Michael's voice softened. "I have a little downtime between projects, and I was thinking of coming up to see you. Could you use some company? I checked some computer travel sites and could be on a flight tomorrow."

"That would be fine." Liza hesitated for a second. "In fact, maybe you could do me a favor. Do you still have my spare set of car keys?"

"They're probably in the back of the junk drawer," Michael said.

"Could you check? I left my car at the Portland Airport. If you come in that way, maybe you could pick it up for the drive here. The long-term parking ticket and the registration are both in the glove compartment."

"That's not the safest place to leave them," Michael said dubiously as he rattled his way through the contents of the junk drawer.

"Safer, I think, than floating around in the bottom of a carry-on bag," Liza replied.

She heard a jingle of keys.

"Okay, got 'em," Michael announced. "Let's just hope the car will be waiting for me."

"That's what I always loved about you, Langley," Liza told him, "that cheerful, upbeat personality."

She got an ETA from him, they said good-bye, and she hung up.

"Okay," she told Rusty. "Back to work. No more telephone calls."

The doorbell rang.

"If this turns out to be Avon calling . . ." Liza muttered as she went to the kitchen door.

But it wasn't—unless Avon had taken to hiring big, bearlike men in khaki police uniforms.

"Sheriff Clements," Liza said in surprise. "What brings you here?"

Even as she spoke, she had a sinking suspicion that the news wouldn't be good.

"There are more questions about what happened yesterday evening at the Redbourne house," Clements told her.

" 'What happened,' " Liza echoed. "Yesterday, you were calling it the suicide at the Redbourne place."

The sheriff nodded. "That's what the questions are about. For example, how did the deceased get up in the air?"

"Chad must have tied off the rope—I'm afraid I didn't notice—probably using the bench in the folly, and then he jumped off," Liza said.

"The problem is, the bench is against the back wall. It's too far away, given the length of rope. Redbourne would have had to set up the rope, then take a flying leap for the noose."

"That doesn't sound likely," Liza slowly said.

Clements nodded in agreement. "And then there's the state of the ground. It had been raining, and that path through the trees isn't paved. If someone had climbed on the cushions, you'd expect a transfer of dirt."

Liza closed her eyes, trying to remember her glance at the bench. The cushions were clean, no dirty footprints.

"Damnation," she muttered. "What else have you got? I can tell from your face that there's something."

"The noose itself," Clements said. "It was just a simple slipknot, not the traditional hangman's knot. Redbourne should have choked to death—a very slow and agonizing way to go."

Liza remembered the sight of Chad's distorted face and shuddered.

"The thing is, Chad caught a break, you might say. He didn't choke; he was killed when the blood flow through the carotid artery was cut off. But the noose didn't do that. The ligature mark that accomplished the job doesn't match the rope around his neck. He was choked garrote style, and then strung up to make it look like a suicide."

"The rope didn't do it?" Liza repeated.

"We're not sure what did," Clements admitted. "It left an odd, regular pattern on his neck . . ."

"Can't you run that through your computers?" Liza asked. "I thought there was a special database . . ."

The sheriff rolled his eyes. "Yeah, that would work fine if this were *CSI: Maiden's Bay*. We'd probably get a hit in five minutes so we could solve the case in an hour minus commercials. Unfortunately, this is real life, so we weren't so lucky—the pattern isn't all that clear. The closest thing we've been able to find is some of the cabling for the outdoor sound system. It has a layer of metal reinforcement wires set within the insulation."

"That would suggest that Chad was strangled out on the terrace," Liza said, almost to herself. "I didn't see any signs of a struggle out there—not that I was looking, of course."

"The only place we're sure of getting any signs is around that artificial cave—what did you call it? The Grotto?" Clements said. "Of course, your little scramble around there with Hagen doesn't help."

"How was I to know . . ." Liza began, but the sheriff raised his hands in a placating gesture.

"I know, I know. It could have been worse. You might have barfed all over the scene."

Before Liza even had a chance to ask, he nodded grimly. "Sometimes discovering a body can be a pretty sickening experience. When I was on the beat back in Portland, I wound up as the first responder for some pretty nasty bits of business. At least then, all I had to do was take one look, get out, and keep anyone else from getting in. As a detective, though, I had to work some pretty gruesome murder scenes—"

He broke off gruffly. "Let's just say vomit doesn't do a heck of a lot for DNA evidence."

Clements rose to his full height, just like a bear catching a new and baffling scent on the breeze. Then he shook his head, impatient with himself. "I'll give this to you straight, Liza. You've been a big help to us in several investigations—investigations that would never have been solved thanks to my inept administration, if you listen to my old friend Oscar Smutz."

He took a deep breath. "But Smutz is out there, this is an election year, and it promises to get pretty dirty. In this case, in spite of my personal opinion about you, my appreciation of what you've done in the past, how much respect I might have for your brains, I've got to treat you like a suspect. I hope you understand."

Shrugging, Clements tried to lighten the mood. "Besides, you don't want that jackass Smutz calling you my crony."

Liza couldn't help smiling. "Right. Sounds too much like 'crone.' "

That at least got a laugh from the sheriff. Then his face got serious. "I'm going to need the shoes and the clothes you were wearing yesterday."

"I hope you don't mind the smell," Liza told him. "I've been soaking them in bleach—"

She broke off at the look on Clements's face. "Sorry," she apologized. "I couldn't resist another CSI joke. The shoes are in the corner over by the door—I was going to scrub off the mud today. The other stuff is up in the laundry hamper."

Retrieving the clothes, Liza came back downstairs. Clements was sealing a plastic evidence bag, with her running shoes inside.

"I hope you don't have to cut them up," Liza said. "They're kind of expensive."

"Shouldn't," the sheriff told her. "Though God knows what the statie techs get up to." He produced a larger bag to receive the bundle of clothing Liza had brought down.

"When I used to go over there, the Redbournes had a white shag rug in the living room. If that's still there, you might get lucky with fibers—not on these," she hastily added.

"I sure as hell hope not," Clements replied. "Just so you know, I sent Curt Walters over to the motel where Clark Hagen is staying, to get the same stuff from him."

Liza nodded, then suddenly said, "You know, Curt used to be on the Killamook High football team."

Clements stopped halfway in turning from the door, the bags dangling from his hands. "You figure he'll have to tackle Hagen?"

She shrugged. "No. It's just that he must have known about the first hanging in the Grotto—the tackling dummy."

"Well, thank you—for your cooperation," Clements said, hefting the evidence bags. "I sincerely hope this will be your last involvement in our investigation."

7

Liza said nothing, giving Clements the "no comment" smile she'd practiced through her years in the publicity biz.

"Stupid," she reproved herself. "Clements will just be after me in a minute."

But the expected knock never came. *Looks as if the sheriff has adopted a "don't ask" policy to go with my "don't tell" one,* she thought

Liza leaned against the shut door, sighing as her eyes took in the view of a kitchen in need of a thorough cleaning.

Why did she even bother to yank Clements's chain like that? No way did she intend to launch her own investigation into this. Chad Redbourne had never been a friend, not even twenty years ago in high school. She'd just felt sorry for the guy.

Well, Chad was well past the point where she could help him now.

She headed for the living room—specifically, the somewhat rickety card table in the corner that held up her computer. Rusty twined himself around her legs a couple of times before she finally sat down. Then he padded off to find the pool of sunlight coming in from the window.

Twice in a circle, and he settled himself comfortably, closing his eyes.

Liza wished it were as easy for her to get started on work. She really didn't have a choice—Ava Barnes would have her hide for a hat if there weren't fresh columns to print.

Turning on the computer, Liza launched the Solv-a-doku program and put a blank sudoku matrix on the screen. A couple of quick keystrokes established one of the symmetrical clue patterns she'd developed earlier.

Let's start off easy, with a nice, simple puzzle, she thought. *Set up a hidden single for 3s here, here . . . and here.*

With the ease of long practice, she inserted 3s into three of the colored clue spaces so that the intersection of their spheres of influence—the columns, rows, and nine-space boxes where their existence prohibited any other 3s—forced the placement of a fourth 3 in one and only one possible spot.

Whistling tunelessly, Liza worked her way through the techniques in the lower half of her twelve steps to sudoku perfection to create a serviceable but simple puzzle.

Liza tried to up her game by creating a more complicated sudoku for her next attempt. Instead she found her attention wandering.

Clearing her work, she began again. But her effort unraveled just as quickly.

With a sigh, Liza hit a few more keys, letting the program shift from puzzle construction mode to playing for a puzzle solution.

Just to clear my head, she thought.

Solv-a-doku spit up a prefab puzzle on the screen, and Liza began trying to solve it. But she quickly lost the thread.

She called up a simpler puzzle and proceeded to screw up that one, too.

"Damn," she muttered. Well, it happened sometimes. Liza called up another puzzle on the same level and did just as badly.

She shrugged and shook her head, trying to loosen up the muscles in her shoulders. Then, grimacing, she grabbed

			9		6			
2		5				9		6
	8						1	
5	7			8			2	4
		4		5				
8	9			3			5	7
	2						6	
9		7				1		8
			8		4			

the computer mouse and went to the games menu, determined to find something else.

Pinball? She never liked that. Minesweeper? No.

She shuddered to discover a game of computerized
Hangman on the list. At last she opened the window for
Spider Solitaire.

It took her three efforts before she finally made it all the
way through the game and cleared the screen.

Liza banged her knuckles in frustration on the tabletop
next to the keyboard, setting the monitor a-jiggle.

"Dammit all," she muttered, killing the game and opening the computer's word processor. Then she typed in
exactly what was distracting her:

WHO KILLED CHAD REDBOURNE?

Under that heading, she began to free-associate.

Somebody at the elections board?

That would make sense. Ted thought there was some funny
business going on there. What if it didn't just involve Chad?

The Killamook machine.

That was the basic reason for the rotten state of elections in the county. Liza's own pseudo-candidacy had come out of the machine's hostility to the threat of reform—or even of change to the status quo—that Ray Massini represented.

But exactly who was involved?

Liza remembered Sheriff Clements's comment that the orders to run her for mayor must have originated somewhere down the hierarchy. Maybe they had even started with Chad, amusing himself by tossing a former classmate into the political mix.

Or it could have come from J.J. Pauncecombe. Certainly, she hadn't had a close personal relationship with him—at the time, Liza would have considered that icky. But maybe the younger Pauncecombe had seen that particular political dirty trick as a slap against Ray Massini and that annoying girl from twenty years ago.

Liza typed in his name, followed by John Jacob Pauncecombe's. It didn't matter if they'd ordered Liza's candidacy or not. The question was Chad's ghost voters, and who might have been implicated if Chad had decided to talk.

Certainly, the Pauncebombes would be at the top of that list.

Who else?

Liza quickly typed "Clark Hagen." Then she frowned. Okay, Hagen had turned up at the scene of the crime right when Liza discovered it, and he'd given her a hell of a scare. He was essentially a mercenary, doing political jobs—even dirty ones—for the highest bidder.

A hired gun, but . . .

I could see him easily engaging in a bit of character assassination, Liza thought. But the real thing?

She let her fingers wander a little farther, and they typed out "Ray Massini."

Liza really scowled at that. Still, Kevin told her that the mayor had been going out of his mind over her supposed candidacy. Liza had figured that Massini would calm down when Kevin reported that it was phony, that she had no intention of running.

But what if he'd decided to take it up with the source of his problems—the county's elections commissioner?

Another name ticked onto the screen—Sheriff Clements. As his visit a while ago showed, he was in the middle of an election campaign, one that worried him.

Could Chad Redbourne have been working behind the scenes to make it more contentious?

She remembered Oscar Smutz standing on the float that was supposed to draw voters to sign petitions for her mayoral run, sneering down at the sheriff. What had he said? "If you got any problems, you can take them up with Mr. Redbourne at the county elections office."

So maybe Clements *did* have a problem with Chad— and had gone for a final resolution.

He had to know that having heard Redbourne's name, Liza would end up paying him a visit. Hell, the man was an investigator. Maybe he even knew that she and Chad had a high school history.

Well, he wouldn't know I'd be heading over to Chad's yesterday evening, Liza thought. *Unless he bugged my phone call with Ava.*

She shook her head. With that kind of paranoid thinking, she might as well start copying out the Killamook County phone book on this screen.

Still . . .

She compromised by putting a question mark after Clements's name.

Then she typed in another name—Oscar Smutz.

He was the one who had mentioned Chad's name, of course, and Liza didn't believe he'd do anything to help either her or Clements. He was involved in the election campaign, too. So if Chad was giving him problems . . .

The guy was crooked, and she really didn't need the sheriff to tell her that. Smutz was also an opportunist. He'd shown that when he hijacked the float meant to bolster her own candidacy.

My fake candidacy, Liza corrected silently.

Then, too, Clements had mentioned that Smutz had been the Killamook machine's go-to guy for police action. Did that include action to plug possible leaks to the state police?

Liza sighed. Casting the net this wide was just another way of saying she had way too many questions and no answers at all.

She put a question mark after Smutz's name, too, then sat up straight as she noticed the time inset on the screen's lower-right-hand corner.

If Michael had managed to get the first flight to Portland, he should be here shortly.

Liza looked down at her walking-the-dog duds.

Maybe I ought to put on something a bit nicer, do up my face—

She heard a car engine in the distance, and then Rusty suddenly shook himself awake, cocking his head. The dog shot Liza a slightly surprised, "What are you doing here?" kind of look.

So the sound of that engine was familiar, one that Rusty knew—like Liza's own car.

The engine stopped, and a moment later, the kitchen doorbell rang. Well, certainly it was someone who knew that the usual entrance to this place was the kitchen and not the front door.

Running a quick hand through her hair to get it into some sort of order, Liza headed for the door and opened it.

There stood Michael Langley, tall and slim, with a poet's face and dark hair with a curl so unruly that it almost took a buzz cut to control it. Right now his large, dark brown eyes looked a little anxious as he said, "Hi, Liza."

The reason for that was the two men standing behind him.

It would be hard to find a pair with a greater contrast. Buck Foreman was tall and beefy, his brown hair short and freshly barbered, his eyes hidden behind a pair of mirrored sunglasses. He still looked like the tough motorcycle cop he'd probably been when he started his career with the LAPD—a look that had served him well as he rose to the detective ranks. He'd certainly intimidated lots of perps and witnesses alike as he investigated a number of high-profile cases.

It hadn't done many favors for him, however, when a defense lawyer found an old tape of Buck making some intemperate remarks. It didn't matter that the tape—and the remarks—had no bearing on the case at hand. By the time the media moved on to the next news item, Buck had wound up as the poster boy for police brutality. He'd had to reinvent himself as a private eye, with help from Michelle Markson. Certainly, he was her PI of choice for dealing with any unsavory business threatening her clients.

The guy standing beside Buck barely came to the private eye's elbow. With his roly-poly body and round, expressive face, Alvin Hunzinger looked as if he'd stepped out of a cartoon. Liza always thought he was the spitting image of Elmer Fudd. But the comical exterior hid one of the sharpest legal minds Liza had ever encountered. Certainly, there was nothing funny about the way Alvin had garnered his title as Lawyer to the Stars. He'd managed to protect many on Hollywood's A-list from the consequences of their own folly—sometimes even when they were innocent.

"Hello, boys." Liza tried not to scowl at her unexpected visitors.

"Sure was a surprise to bump into them at the airport," Michael quickly said, trying to disavow any knowledge of their actions. A bit of pique did shine through as he added, "Of course, they were riding business class, while I was in coach."

"Anyway, Michael was kind enough to offer us a lift down here," Alvin began, but he stopped at the look on Liza's face.

Actually, it wasn't anger, but the attempt to hold in a laugh. She'd have paid money to see the three of them trying to emerge from her compact car. It would be like watching one of those clown cars in the circus.

"I, ah, take it that Michelle didn't happen to mention

we were on the way?" Alvin added nervously. He might be utterly fearless in the courtroom, but when Michelle Markson told Alvin to jump, he only wanted to know how high.

"Probably saw it as a waste of time," Buck Foreman said in his rumbling bass voice.

Liza had to hand it to the PI. Buck showed unexpected depths of diplomacy, leaving the question open as to whether it would be wasting Michelle's time to give Liza any kind of warning, or whether the waste would be Liza's trying to argue with Michelle once the senior partner had made up her mind.

"She probably just wanted to make sure I didn't go on vacation again before you got here." Realizing that was ungracious, Liza stood aside in the doorway. "Well, come on in. I've got coffee on, and I'm sure you must be dehydrated after your flight."

She left Rusty to greet the guests in the living room while she went into the kitchen to arrange a tray.

Michael trailed after her.

"I really didn't know about any of this until I found Foreman looming over me at the gate in the airport terminal."

"He is pretty good at looming, isn't he?" Liza headed back into the living room with her tray. "I've got to tell you what a warm, fuzzy feeling it gives me to see you guys come all this way—even if Michelle made you do it. But I think it's a lot of effort for nothing. I'm not intending to investigate—"

"Sure, of course. It's obvious," Foreman rumbled from his spot in front of her computer, where he stood reading the screen. "You have no interest at all."

Liza scowled. *Damn detectives, always sticking their noses in where they aren't wanted,* she thought.

"I didn't say I have no interest," she replied testily. "I said I wasn't going to investigate. The sheriff was here this morning, and he came out and asked me not to—"

"That might be because he considers you a suspect," Alvin interrupted. "You had a public difference of opinion with Chad Redbourne, and it ended with a fairly provocative threat from you."

"Provocative?" Liza echoed.

"You mentioned swinging—and not in a good way."

The memory of her exit from Chad's office came back—standing in the doorway and saying, "Someone's going to swing."

Liza looked around at her friends. "Well, it was just something to say." Her lips twisted. "Yeah, pretty lame. But he'd just about blown me off, and I wanted some kind of a comeback—"

She broke off. "You don't think that gave somebody the idea . . ."

"I just think you should consider self-defense," Alvin said.

Buck stared at him. "Interesting plea—I don't think I've ever heard of a person hanging someone in self-defense before."

Now it was Alvin's turn to stare. "I didn't mean that as a plea. I meant that Liza should defend herself against accusation by taking action—finding a viable alternative."

"You mean, investigating the case," Michael translated.

Foreman grinned. "Come on, you know you want to do it."

"I don't." Liza plumped down on the sofa. "I didn't much care for Chad back in high school, and the first time I see him after twenty years, he acts like a weasel and just about lies to my face."

"And then somebody strings him up," Michael said.

Liza sighed. "All right, I suppose we can do a little brainstorming. But I think we'd better call Kevin Shepard."

Michael's eyes narrowed. "Why do you need him?"

"*We* need him," Liza replied, "for his local knowledge and the political stuff he's been privy to as a friend of Ray Massini. If I could do it, I'd have Ava Barnes here, too—except she'd probably be trying to put our faces on the front page of the *Oregon Daily*."

She didn't mention why she wanted Kevin to come over, even when he innocently asked if he should bring his toolbox. While they waited for him, they discussed Liza's list. Buck Foreman was surprisingly diplomatic in suggesting that Liza's suspicions rested more on guesswork than logic. Hell, Liza agreed with him.

When Kevin arrived, he took one look at Buck, Alvin, and Michael, raised a hand to his ear, and said, "Whoops, I think I hear my mother calling."

"We need your help." Liza took a deep breath. "I need your help. We've got a mess here that no toolbox can fix."

"It is a mess," Kevin agreed glumly.

"I guess your friend Ray must be glad to hear that Liza isn't really running for mayor," Alvin said.

"He's relieved," Kevin replied. "Ray said people are crazy enough over celebrities without getting them into politics."

"And he doesn't have any other beef with Redbourne?" Buck asked.

Kevin looked at him. "You don't think Ray had anything to do with what happened, do you? He wouldn't mind seeing Redbourne and a lot of other drones out of their jobs, but he's not about to put on a mask and go around stringing them up."

"So the news is out that Chad's death wasn't a suicide," Liza said.

"Yeah, it came out on KMUC after the morning chucklefest was over." Kevin shook his head. "I always felt kind of bad about Redbourne. You know how all through school, J.J. Pauncecombe was on his back? Well, he wanted all the other guys on the team to go after Chad, too. I did some pretty nasty stuff to the guy, just to go along with the team."

"Like the hanged tackling dummy?" Liza asked.

"That was J.J.," Kevin told her. "It's funny how, in the end, Chad wound up working for J.J.'s old man."

"Not as strange as what happened with J.J.'s girlfriend." The words burst out almost before Liza realized she'd said them.

Kevin gave her a funny look. "Why would you mention that?"

Because even after twenty years, that witch still gives me hives, Liza thought. Aloud, she said, "I just thought it was weird, her marrying the old man."

Kevin gave an uncomfortable shrug. "I dunno. There were always stories about Brandy and older guys."

Liza remembered the old high school gossip. Brandy and upperclassmen, Brandy and college guys. There were even some rumors going around that almost cost the JV football coach his job. "I don't suppose she was ever tight with Ray Massini?"

Kevin started to shake his head, but then had to shrug. "I really don't know, although I don't think so," he said. "But I can tell one story you might find interesting.

"It was right back when the inn first opened. I'd make it a point every evening to hit the dining room at dinnertime and greet all the guests."

He still does that, Liza thought.

"Anyway, I go in one night, and who's there but Chad and Brandy Pauncecombe." Kevin laughed. "It was kind of funny. Chad was pouring a bottle of wine, and when he spotted me, he got that same expression he used to get when he saw J.J. bearing down on him. He completely spazzed out, spilling wine on the tablecloth. I guess I must have been about the last person on earth he expected to see there."

"Brandy—and Chad?" Liza said in disbelief.

Kevin nodded, still grinning at the memory. "Never saw a guy eat so fast. He just about hustled Brandy out of there. I was at the front desk when they left."

Here his grin faded a little. "Here's the really weird thing. The desk clerk mentioned that when they came in, Chad had been pricing the cost of a room."

8

Michael, of course, had a scriptwriter's take on this development. "So, twenty years after high school, the class nerd and the prom queen get together—and get it on!"

"This isn't a pitch meeting," Liza told him irritably. "And Brandy wasn't the prom queen—more like the school slut." She turned to Kevin. "Wasn't she?"

"Well, uh . . ." Kevin said, taken aback.

"I can't believe you want to be nice to her!" Liza burst out.

"Wow, twenty years and it's still . . ." Michael made a clawing gesture with one hand while letting out an angry cat noise that was realistic enough to make Rusty raise his head from his doze by the window.

"She was a selfish, two-faced, backstabbing bitch who never told the truth if a lie suited her purposes better—or maybe just amused her."

"Sounds like the perfect politician's wife," Buck Foreman suggested with a grin.

Alvin, however, looked more serious. "I think you've just shown how the passions from all those years ago could still live on today."

Liza blinked, shut up, and thought. "We all remember how J.J. Pauncecombe made life hell for Chad," she said to Kevin. "But do you remember why?"

He shrugged. "Because Chad was always around."

"Because Chad was always around Brandy," Liza corrected. "That's what drove J.J. crazy, having some geeky guy carrying a torch for Brandy."

Kevin reluctantly nodded. "And no matter what J.J. did to him, Chad kept coming back."

"Puppy love," Liza said, then frowned. "Do you think Chad could have kept holding the torch all those years?"

"He never got married," Kevin pointed out.

"Of course, there was the other side to it." Liza could hear the sharper note creeping into her voice. "Back in school, Brandy liked having Chad looking all googly-eyed at her."

"Flattered by the attention?" Michael suggested. "Maybe he had more to offer than some high school jock." He glanced over at Kevin as he said this.

Liza rolled her eyes. *Here we go again.* Aloud, she said, "I wonder if Brandy ever had an honest emotion in her life. I think she just liked the drama. When nobody else much was around, she'd lead Chad on—smile at him or whatever—until J.J. came along to open a can of whup-ass on the poor sucker."

"And he used to order cans of whup-ass by the case," Kevin said. "Very heavy with his hands, old J.J. was. I think he managed to get into a fight with everybody on the team."

"Well, that was an interesting trip down memory lane," Buck commented. "But it's interesting mainly because it raises a possible motive other than election fraud. Do you think we could get hold of pictures of Redbourne and this woman—something a little more up to date than yearbook photos?"

Kevin nodded. "I've got some pictures from political dinners held at the inn—"

"Rubber chicken and oratory," Michael murmured just loud enough to be heard.

Kevin bristled, but Buck cut in. "Maybe you could go

and get them—even better, maybe you could e-mail them to Liza's computer."

"I have a scanner in my office." Kevin rose from his seat. "I'll see what I can do."

After he'd left, Liza asked Buck, "What do you intend to do with those pictures?"

Buck shrugged, an infinitesimal lift of his heavy shoulders. "I'll make the rounds of motels in the area."

Too bad we didn't ask Kevin about that, Liza thought. *He's probably researched all the no-tell motels in easy driving range for his pal Ray.*

But then, nobody was supposed to know about that. She was glad she'd kept her mouth shut.

Turning to Alvin, she said, "Well, Buck has figured out something to do. But I really feel that you've been dragged off on a wild-goose chase."

Alvin shook his round, bald head. "I'd been intending to take a few days off, and I would have ended up wasting them on golf. This is something different for me. Usually, I get called in when someone is pretty sure to be arrested or indicted. It isn't often I get to do some preventive lawyering."

Liza shrugged, flinging up her hands in defeat. "Okay, then, the next thing we have to do is figure out a place for you to stay. I don't suppose Michelle is willing to pick up the tab—"

Buck shook his head. "I think she's drawing the line at getting us up here, and even then, it was done on frequent flyer miles."

Liza grinned. That was classic Michelle.

"So I guess rooms at the Killamook Inn are out."

"Not to mention a little too open to the public," Buck said. "If your local sheriff didn't want you investigating, I figure maybe we should keep our presence on the down low."

Looking at her three guests, Liza sighed. "Well, Mrs. H. has a guest room next door, but that would be awfully cramped for more than one person."

"I seem to remember she also has a good-sized couch," Buck said. "I could crash there."

It could be done—Kevin had lain there, passed out in the course of one case. She glanced over at Michael. While he had lain passed out on the floor.

"I guess you can stay here," she told Michael. Then, to quench the sudden twinkle in his eyes, she added, "I think there's still an old sleeping bag stuck in with Dad's camping things."

Ignoring the look on Michael's face, Liza went to the living room window. "Mrs. H. has her Olds parked beside the house," she said. "Let's go next door and talk with her."

Mrs. Halvorsen opened the door with a smile. "Hello, hello!" she said. "I'm glad to see you up here visiting, Michael. And it's always a pleasure to see you, Mr. Foreman." She had to tilt her head back to look Buck in the eye.

"Elise Halvorsen, Alvin Hunzinger," Liza introduced the final member of the group. "He came down to the resort where we were staying, but I don't think you had a chance to meet then."

Mainly because Alvin was busy getting her away from the police and a media frenzy while Mrs. H. hid in their room.

The older woman's eyes widened as she stared at Alvin. "Has anybody mentioned how much you look like . . ."

Seeing the way Alvin cringed, Liza figured she wasn't the only one to notice his resemblance to old Elmer, even if she hadn't mentioned it out loud.

"That actor from *Kojak*," Mrs. H. went on. "What was his name? Telly something . . ."

"Savalas?" Michael blurted out in astonishment.

"That's it." Mrs. Halvorsen nodded vigorously. "Telly Savalas. I always thought he was a dangerous-looking type, even when he played good guys. If that nice Mr. Foreman weren't here with you, I'd have been afraid to open the door."

"Really?" Alvin deepened his voice. "I mean, really." Squaring his shoulders, he straightened to his full, if not very considerable, height. "Who loves ya, baby?"

Mrs. H. clapped her hands. "Exactly!"

She expressed herself as more than willing to put up Buck and his famous-looking friend.

"Great," Buck said. "We'll just go and get our bags."

On the way back from the car, though, Buck detoured back to Liza's house. "I wonder if Kevin was able to get the stuff we asked for this quickly," he said.

She went inside and switched to the Internet. And yes, she had mail.

Printing out the attachments, she handed them to Buck. "A little blurry," Liza said, looking at them critically.

"Probably blown up from a group picture." Buck held the pictures out. "He's wearing a tux, and her gown must be cut down to the belly button."

Both Michael and Alvin clustered around for a peek, each earning a dirty look from Liza.

"But I think they'll do," Buck told her. "How are they in terms of likeness?"

She looked at the tight, nervous smile on Chad's face and the way Brandy was busy making love to the camera. "Good likenesses, and very much in character."

Buck folded the photos and put them in his jacket pocket. "Now, if I wanted to arrange a discreet rendezvous, where would I start looking?"

Liza bit her lip to keep from answering, "Try the Killamook Inn."

Instead, she said, "There are a lot of touristy motels along the coast to the north, up to Seaside and Cannon Beach. Or south along the coast, there's Lincoln City and Newport."

Buck nodded. "I'm going to need a car—and I don't think it would be a good idea to rent one." He gave Liza a humorless smile. "Less of a paper trail."

"Well, I'd willingly lend you mine, but I've been carless for days now, and I have things to take care of."

"Wonder if your neighbor would let me borrow her car, then," Buck said.

"I'm sure she would," Liza assured him. "Let's go and ask."

They returned with Buck to Mrs. H.'s house and made the necessary arrangements. Buck would head north, Alvin would stay and enjoy his newfound celebrity, and Liza and Michael would get some time alone.

"So what are you intending to do with your newly returned car?" Michael asked.

"I figured I'd fill the gas tank—and then we'd do something we haven't done in a long time," Liza replied.

Her almost-ex-husband's eyebrows rose nearly to his hairline. "Like what?"

She smiled. "Like go on a picnic."

The first stop was Castelli's Market a few blocks away, where they got a six-pack of beer, assorted sodas, and some of the homemade Italian delicacies the store was famous for. Michael went for the veal parmigiana hero with extra sauce. Liza chose her usual—prosciutto, capicola, salami, and provolone cheese, with lettuce, tomato, balsamic vinegar, and marinated peppers. Ernie behind the counter alerted Liza as to which pasta salad was the freshest, and they took a tub of that, too.

Having gotten fuel for themselves, they headed for the edge of town and a service station, where Liza gassed up the car.

"Where to now?" Michael asked.

"We head for the hills," Liza replied, taking a winding road that quickly took on elevation.

"Damn," Liza muttered after they'd been driving for a while. "We forgot ice."

"It shouldn't be so bad." Michael twisted against his seat belt to feel the beverages on the floor of the backseat. "Um. Maybe we should have separated the hot sandwich from the stuff we'd like to keep cold."

"No problem—maybe. We're near Hillside Road." Liza made a left at the next intersection, turning onto a slightly wider road that looped in splendid isolation along the flank of the hillside to a wider shoulder of flattish ground. It had been graded and covered in gravel to form a parking area, presently home to a single battered pickup truck pulled up

in front of a glorified shed that sprouted like a dusty cinderblock mushroom. A sign in peeling paint over the door
announced the single word CONVENIENCE.

Michael peered at the slit-like windows while waiting
for the cloud of dust from their approach to settle down.
"So what is it? A leftover fallout shelter or the supply point
for all the local hermits?"

Liza shrugged. "It was going to be a construction shanty
for a housing development, but between foot-dragging by
the boys in Killamook and the present economy, that's
all that got built." She led the way inside, where a whip-
thin man with a dark complexion and a magnificent mus-
tache bowed from behind the counter. "How may I be of
assistance?"

"Hello, Mr. Patel," Liza said. "Do you have any ice?"

The shopkeeper nodded to a row of refrigerated cases
against the far wall. "Look in the one on the end."

Michael followed along behind Liza, taking in the
store's inventory—snack foods, chilled beer and soda, a
few containers of milk, display units with aspirin, cold
pills, pain rubs, and various digestive nostrums standing
next to bottles of motor oil, transmission fluid, and other
automotive necessities. Beside the last cooler, where Liza
dug out a plastic bag of ice, the merchandise changed character again, this time to stationery items. Beyond rose a
rank of private mailboxes, three bays of them from letter
to parcel size.

Michael let out a muffled "Ooof!" as Liza shoved the
ten-pound bag of ice into his arms to carry and made
almost the same sound when he saw how much she had to
pay for it.

"Anything to pay the rent," he muttered when they were
back outside, "and everything the market will bear."

"As the sign says, we're paying for convenience." Liza
held open the back door as Michael dumped his burden
on the drinks. "This isn't exactly a well-traveled road. I'm
surprised Mr. Patel manages to stay in business."

They got in the car, retraced their route, and then

continued up the hill. Soon they arrived at Liza's favorite picnic spot. A copse of trees provided shade while the elevation offered an amazing view of the town and the bay in the distance.

Liza spread an old blanket right at the edge of sunlight while Michael lugged over the bag of ice. "This thing has frozen into one big mass," he complained.

"Just drop it a few times."

While he did that, she went back to the car, returning with the toolbox from the trunk.

"I think it's in three pieces now," Michael puffed as he bent to pick up the bag again.

Liza dropped to her knees and opened the box, removing a utility knife and a screwdriver. She slit the plastic, spread it, and then began attacking the frozen masses, using the screwdriver as an improvised ice pick. "Why don't you bring over the drinks?"

When Michael returned, she set the bottles in the chopped ice and then rose to retrieve the rest of their lunch.

"There, now," she said, setting the sandwiches and salad down beside Michael, who was already sprawled on the blanket. She poked a toe in his ribs. "Shift over."

He made room, and she joined him on the blanket, hip to hip. "We're lucky. If those developers had gotten their way, this would probably be the front lawn of a luxury residence for some family from California."

"I thought you guys really hated those interlopers from California."

Liza shrugged. "They're a fact of life . . . and they help to spread the tax bill a bit farther around. Pauncecombe and his cronies have turned Killamook into Disneyland on the Bay. They want to maintain the status quo, and that's expensive, as I found when I took over the property taxes for the house in Maiden's Bay. Not to mention that the Killamook machine keeps siphoning off funds for their own purposes."

"I guess it's true," Michael said. "You *can't* go home

again." He looked over at Liza. "And it looks as if revisiting your past may not be much fun, either."

"Some people look back on high school as the most wonderful time of their lives." Liza shook her head. "I'm not one of them. Too much petty BS—and yes, Brandy D'Alessandro was often the one who was dishing it out. Now I see her with her perfect boobs, showing off her tiny waist with a gold belt, and she's probably paying for it with money her husband sucked out of my taxes."

Michael snaked his hand into the bag of ice. "I think there's only one cure when you get that hot under the collar. And luckily, I think the beer is cool enough now."

He extracted a bottle, twisted off the cap, and handed it to Liza. "Keep on like this, and you'll end up with no appetite for your sandwich."

"I was hoping we could trade halves," Liza said and then took a sip.

It took some additional negotiation, but Michael finally agreed to swap half his sandwich. They took their time eating, and Liza switched to soda after she finished her first beer.

And for a long while they just lay in companionable silence on the blanket, looking up at the sky through the branches overhead.

"The only thing we lack is music," Michael said, stretching lazily. "My folks used to pack a transistor radio with our picnic lunches."

"With my luck, all we'd get is KMUC, and we're coming up to the Blowhard Hour."

Michael turned to her. "Blowhard Hour?"

"They've got some low-rent political pundit who pontificates and takes phone calls. He might as well be the minister of propaganda for the Killamook machine."

She decided to demonstrate after they'd cleaned up and gotten back in the car, tuning in the local station.

"Any other callers with comments on the upcoming primaries?" a very self-assured voice inquired from the speakers.

A much more pugnacious voice followed, with that slight fuzziness that seems to accompany phone calls over the airwaves. "Len, this is Oscar Smutz, candidate for sheriff."

Liza made a disgusted noise. This didn't seem like a joke or impersonation. It sounded just like Smutz's speech-making style from the hijacked campaign float.

"I don't have a question about the election so much as about local crime."

Liza's hand headed for the dial to turn this nonsense off as Smutz asked, "Why is Sheriff Clements shielding his friend Liza Kelly in the Redbourne murder investigation?"

9

Liza jerked back her hand as if a fat blue spark had just jumped from the radio control. "What's this moron talking about?"

But as she and Michael listened, Oscar Smutz outlined his case.

"It's bad enough that the county has been involved in three high-profile murder cases and the theft of a multimillion-dollar artwork, but the present sheriff turned out to be incompetent in solving them. The killers would have escaped and the painting never been found if Liza Kelly hadn't handed Bert Clements the answers on a silver platter. And even then it ended badly—the sheriff muffed an arrest attempt, standing uselessly by as trigger-happy deputies killed a third-generation merchant in Maiden's Bay."

Liza made a disgusted noise back in her throat. Smutz's blathering was true after a fashion, or rather a truth sandwich—a few very thin facts with a lot of dirt and innuendo crammed in between.

If Liza had managed to solve some of the crimes Smutz was yelling about, she wouldn't have been able to do it without the help of Bert Clements. He had shared information and even pointed her in directions to get information where a cop couldn't go.

But Smutz kept ranting on. "Now it looks as though Kelly thinks she's won herself a free pass. Or is Clements just afraid of a celebrity? She was heard threatening a guy who turned up dead a few hours later. And when the cops arrive at the scene of the crime, who's standing there? Liza Kelly. Now, I've spent a few years as a cop, and what I just said would put her down as a suspect in my book. Does Clements bring her downtown? No, he goes to visit her house."

"Clements came to collect my clothes for forensics. He also sent a deputy to Hagen's motel for the same reason. He already had our statements and was checking them out." She ground her words out between gritted teeth.

Michael rested a gentle hand on her shoulder. "Do you often carry on arguments with your radio?" he asked.

She sighed and turned off the damned thing. "I suppose you're right—and I also suppose we'd better get back to Buck and Alvin. We'll be making plans tonight—and if I don't miss my guess, we'll be getting a call from Michelle, too."

They got back to Hackleberry Avenue and went over to Mrs. Halvorsen's house. Buck was still gone, but Alvin had apparently been listening to the radio. "It looks as though Michelle was right to send me up here." His round, comical-looking face was set in serious lines. "Don't be surprised if the sheriff calls you in."

"What more can he expect to get from me?" Liza demanded.

"He can expect to get this Smutz character off his back," Alvin replied. "You're in the publicity end of things, Liza. He's making some colorful charges that tie into a big murder case."

Liza nodded, her lips twisting. "Yeah, I expect other news outlets will pick it up."

She was only too right. By the time Buck finally showed up, Smutz was appearing on the local newscast from

Lincoln City. If she'd been watching on her own TV, Liza might have been tempted to put a foot through the screen. But they were watching on Mrs. H.'s old console, so she had to contain herself.

The extra twenty pounds that the camera adds were especially evident on Smutz's face. With his doughy cheeks and missing neck, he looked like an outraged bullfrog as he continued his attacks against Clements and Liza.

"Oh, Michelle's not going to be happy with this," Buck said, watching the performance.

"Right now, I'm more concerned with hearing if you have anything interesting to say," Liza told him.

"Matrimonial work isn't really something I get into, so I can't say I made an exhaustive search," Foreman replied. "But if our young lovers sought afternoon delight—or any other kind—they either didn't head north or were extremely circumspect."

"Well, they can't have been too careful if Shepard caught on to them," Michael said.

"Caught on to whom?" Mrs. Halvorsen asked.

Liza cleared her throat a little nervously, trying to keep it clean for the grandmotherly woman. "We think that Chad Redbourne—the fellow who was murdered—might have been having an affair with Brandy Pauncecombe."

"You mean the D'Alessandro girl?" Mrs. H. nodded, her lips pursed. "I've heard some stories along those lines."

Liza gawked. "You have?" Then she shut her mouth. Of course, if anybody were to hear anything, it would be Elise Halvorsen, one of the champion gossips in Maiden's Bay.

"Not that it comes as much of a surprise, I suppose," Mrs. H. went on. "Brandy was always a fairly . . . red-blooded girl, tied to a much older man. To tell the truth, I always felt a little sorry for her. They didn't exactly marry for love, but now she's trapped in a social circle where everyone is old enough to be her mother or her father."

The idea of sympathy for Brandy was more than Liza could stomach. "And that's enough for her to fall madly in bed with Chad Redbourne?"

"I've heard his name mentioned, along with others," her neighbor replied. "Some of them more shocking than that."

"Oh, really?" Foreman said. "I'll have to go over some of that with you—"

He didn't get to finish because Liza's cell phone began to ring.

"Now you see why I decided to stay away from handling politicians," Michelle Markson said in Liza's ear. "Too many publicity variables to deal with. Although I thought that the help I sent you should have headed off any problems."

The very mildness of her voice was enough to raise a "Run for your life!" red flag for any veteran of the Markson wars.

"Now I understand that two of the larger Portland network affiliates are arranging interviews to allow this Schmuck person to bad-mouth you." There were those incredibly sensitive media antennas Michelle was famous for. Liza listened as her partner's voice grew even more deceptively mild. "I'd hoped that Alvin would have dispensed with any problems from your friend the sheriff."

Liza foresaw Michelle making pure hell out of Alvin's life if she didn't speak up. "We—*I*—thought the problems had already been dealt with."

Michelle responded with an impatient sigh. "Really, Liza. You may not have dealt with politics at the agency, but I assumed your defensive game would be better than this."

Liza braced herself for the blast to begin, but instead Michelle just said, "It looks as if I'll have to deal with these politicians myself. Luckily, I had the staff here doing research since we first heard about your latest escapade."

Only Michelle would consider stumbling across a dead body as an "escapade."

"Does that mean you're coming up here?" Liza asked apprehensively. Sheriff Clements had already dealt with Alvin in the past and wouldn't be very happy to see him again. The sheriff had also met Michelle, and Liza suspected he wasn't exactly eager to renew that acquaintance, either.

"No, I think I can be more effective right here in the office," Michelle told her.

"And what are you going to do?" Liza found even more apprehension coming on.

"It might be best if you don't know the specifics." Michelle's voice went to a malicious purr. "Just remember, the best defense is a strong offense."

Michelle cut the connection, and Liza gloomily clicked her phone shut to find all eyes on her.

"I take it Herself was not pleased," Michael said.

"She felt our brain trust should have anticipated this particular can of worms," Liza admitted.

"Oh, God." Alvin seemed to shrink in upon himself, lines of anxiety appearing all over his round face. Liza had seen similar expressions on most of the people who regularly worked with Michelle and her take-no-prisoners business style. Despite the fat retainers that he'd pocketed through the Markson Agency, Alvin Hunzinger's personal relationship with Michelle seemed based more on terror than greed.

"Looks as though it's going to be you and me this evening, Alvin," Liza told the attorney. "Even if Clements doesn't bring me in, I'll have to go see him—see if we can kick this thing out of the news cycle as quickly as possible. The problem is, I'll have to go in there alone."

Alvin stiffened, immediately opening his mouth to object. Of course, if Liza's plan went wrong, Michelle would want his head for a lawn ornament.

Liza brought her hand up in a "stop" gesture. "If I go in lawyered up, this will turn into an adversarial thing with Clements and the cops. Also, you have a certain celebrity quality of your own, Alvin—you've got a rep for helping guilty people walk on all sorts of charges. We don't want the media or the political types making that sort of connection."

"I—understand." But Alvin didn't look happy.

"If there's trouble, though, you'll be the lawyer I'll call," Liza promised with a smile.

Her good mood faded as she punched in the number for police headquarters in Killamook. Clements was still in his office, and his voice sounded a little relieved as he came on the line. "I was going to wait until morning."

"Well, let's set the time and get this over with," Liza said. "I hope you'll at least have a clean rubber hose on hand."

"Right." Clements didn't sound ready to join in the joke. "Shall we say eleven o'clock?"

"Eleven o'clock it will be," Liza told him. She said good-bye and closed her phone.

Then she took a deep breath, her eyes going to Buck Foreman. "I guess you'll be involved in this, too. We'll have to make it as tough a grilling as possible on my statement." Liza shrugged. "At least I have the advantage of being innocent."

Hours later, that didn't seem like much of an advantage anymore. Buck Foreman didn't just lead her through the events of the fatal afternoon, he raked Liza over the coals.

"After I left Chad, I had coffee with Ted Everard, a state cop," she told the private eye. "Doesn't that count for anything?"

Buck wasn't impressed, while Alvin actively worried. "Some people could see that as an attempt to set up an alibi."

They continued through the course of events—going to the kennel to pick up Rusty, and then going home and bumping into Kevin. Michael got very interested in that, although Liza managed to keep Ray Massini's name out of the encounter. Then came her phone conversations with Michelle and Ava, followed by Liza popping over to Mrs. H. to ask if she could use her neighbor's Oldsmobile again.

"Do I still sound guilty?" Liza couldn't quite keep the pleading note from her voice as she looked at Alvin.

He sat in silence for a moment. Then Alvin spoke to Buck. "The telephone calls can be checked exactly, and I suppose the state police sergeant can be reasonably exact on time." Then he turned to Liza. "How busy was the kennel? Would the young woman there have a firm idea of the time? You were still in the other town—Killamook—then." Back to Buck. "Do we know when the victim left work? Time of death? We want to make sure there's no window of opportunity when Liza might have stopped off on the way home to kill Redbourne."

Foreman consulted his notes. "They don't have a solid time of death—still waiting on the coroner. Redbourne left his office a little early, but I think, considering the time it would take to string up the corpse . . ." He shook his head. "I guess it would depend on how firm Shepard is regarding her arrival around here."

Great, Liza thought. *Given the state he was in, I don't think he was checking his watch when I came driving up.*

"On the other end," Buck said, "Liza, did you do your shopping at a supermarket or a small store?"

"Since I had the car, I drove to the big supermarket on the edge of town," she answered.

"Good. A big operation probably means security cameras, and maybe a time-stamped picture of you pushing a shopping cart around."

"And when I popped in on Mrs. H., she was watching one of her game shows. *Jeopardy,* I think. She should remember, and that will give an idea of when I left for the store."

Alvin nodded. "The other end of the timeline lies with this political operative—what was his name?"

"Clark Hagen," Liza and Buck both said.

"Well, they'll have the dueling 911 calls," Liza added.

"Right," Foreman said tonelessly. "Let's go over this again . . ."

The next morning, Liza gave a low groan as her alarm went off. It was earlier than she usually liked to get up, but she didn't want to be rushing around. She rose, showered, and put some thought into the clothes she put on. Liza didn't want to go as far as the Armani suit in the zip-up canvas bag at the end of the closet, but she didn't want to go in looking like a ragpicker, either.

"Very nice," Michael said from his nest of sheets on the couch. When they returned from Mrs. Halvorsen's the night before, he'd just gone to the linen closet and started arranging a bed for himself. "After what you just went through, I figure the last thing you need is pleasure—er, pressure," he'd said.

"Freudian slip," she'd told him then, plodding up the stairs.

Now Liza asked, "Coffee?"

Michael stretched and pushed himself up on one elbow. "Yes, please." He hesitated for a moment. "Want me to go with?"

"I went back and forth over that at least three times in the shower," Liza admitted. "And my final choice is—no. I don't think I want to go in there with an entourage—or even a husband."

"Well, I guess I can take it easy here . . ." Michael broke off as Rusty trotted up to look at him nose to nose. A second later, the dog jumped back in alarm when Michael let out a thunderous sneeze.

Sighing—and then sneezing again—Michael swung round to sit up. "Where did I leave those allergy pills?"

While he went off in search of them, Liza headed for the coffeemaker in the kitchen. The rich smell of coffee filled the room as Michael reappeared, a large blue pill in one hand, the other over his mouth and nose. His brown eyes disappeared for a moment as his whole face scrunched up. Then he shook his head. "Don't you hate it when you're about to sneeze, and it doesn't come?"

A second later, the sneeze did come, startling Rusty again.

Liza filled a mug and handed it to Michael, who immediately took the pill and a sip.

"Toast?" he asked, heading for the loaf of rye bread.

"Yeah, I think that's all I need." She patted her stomach. "Butterflies."

Soon, she, Michael, and Rusty were fed. Liza kept the dog on a reel-in leash as he dashed out to do his business. Then she went back upstairs to put on her face. As she brushed her hair, Liza saw a bit more of a chestnut gleam thanks to her time in the sun.

"All right," she told her reflection in the mirror. "Here we go."

Liza banged a fist against her steering wheel in frustration as she headed downtown on Main Street. "Where the hell is this traffic coming from?" she muttered. "This isn't rush hour on the 405. It's eleven freaking o'clock."

Maybe she should have turned on the radio for a traffic report. But she couldn't stomach the idea of listening to the maunderings of the Killamook Krew.

In two blocks, she got a clue when she spotted a police cruiser parked on the side of the road. Deputy Brenna Ross waved her over. "Sheriff sent me here when the TV trucks started gathering in front of City Hall," she said. "If you want, I can take you around back . . ."

But Liza shook her head. "I can't say I like it, but when you come down to it, seeing me go in is the purpose of the exercise."

She ended up parking a couple of blocks from City Hall and then walked into the crowd. It took a few moments for the newspeople to recognize her. She was actually mounting the steps before the cameras aimed and the bombardment of silly-ass questions began.

"What did you have against Chad Redbourne?"

"Was it a sick joke to hang Chad?"

"Are you really running for mayor?"

Liza had already schooled her face into a calm, mild mask. When she reached the door, she turned and gave her prepared statement. "The sheriff has asked me to come

in and expand on my statement. I am happy to assist his
investigation."

Ignoring the storm of questions, she went inside.

The actual interrogation went much more gently than the
practice ones Buck Foreman had conducted. They sat in the
small room that doubled as the sheriff's office when he was
in town. Liza noticed that a cassette recorder was set up on
the table and the chair with one short leg, usually reserved for
people being questioned, was occupied by Bert Clements.

He clicked on the recorder, giving the date and time,
identifying himself and Liza. Then the questions began.
When he was done, he thanked Liza, then turned the
recorder off.

"And I mean thank you, Liza," Clements said. "For
this—this—"

"Bit of political theater?" Liza asked.

The sheriff grimaced. "That's as good a name as any. Lord,
how I hate this political crap. I think I'm a good cop, but I'd
rather face some nut with a gun than another speech."

"Isn't being a good cop what got you elected?" Liza said.

"I got elected because my predecessor screwed up,"
Clements told her.

Liza basically remembered the former sheriff from
parades and school visits as a kid. Newt McFarland had
always worn a uniform more suited to the supreme poten-
tate of some dictatorship, the fancy tailoring forced to deal
with a figure growing steadily more portly. He stood in
startling contrast to Clements's plain khakis, distinguished
from the deputies only by a gold badge.

"Newt was a cop who did a good job of keeping the
streets clean and the budget balanced," Clements said.
"Police and criminal justice soaks up about a quarter of
the twenty million bucks the country runs on each year."

He shook his head. "But in the end, Newt got a little
crazy over the way everybody else seemed to be lining their
pockets. So he went out of the county to expand our cruiser
fleet—and tried to get a kickback from a car dealer being
investigated by the staties for tax fraud. The guy rolled on

him to get a lighter sentence, and Killamook needed a new sheriff—preferably one without any political ties."

"Someone like you," Liza said. "And you've done a good job."

"Yeah, but now voters have forgotten about Newt. And some folks in the machine figure they should exercise better 'control.'"

"Especially over that five-million-dollar budget, I bet." Liza's voice got a bit more tart. "But somebody like Oscar Smutz?"

Clements shrugged. "He jumped to get out in front first. If he uses the murder case to make me look bad enough, he might get the nod. But if in doing that, he gets too much attention put on what Chad was doing for the machine, the boys in Killamook won't know him. Either way, I'm going to take some lumps."

He rose to open the door and found the desk deputy waiting for him. "The memorial for Mr. Redbourne has been pushed up to tonight," the man reported. "Six thirty at Freney's Funeral Home."

Liza blinked. "Did the coroner even release Chad's remains?"

Sheriff Clements shook his head. "And when they do, his parents want the remains shipped to Arizona. But if John Jacob and associates can't bury Chad physically, they'll do it politically."

Liza snuck out the back door of City Hall and walked home unnoticed. She asked Michael to head downtown and recover her car. Then, aside from lunch, she worked on pieces for her column.

Late in the afternoon, though, she took a shower and looked in her closet to resurrect another work outfit—one in a dark color.

"Whoa!" Michael sat up straight on the couch, where he'd been reading printouts of Liza's new columns. "Are we going out to dinner?"

"No," Liza replied, "I'm going to crash the Killamook machine's farewell to Chad Redbourne."

10

When Liza opened the door, however, she found her way blocked by the tall, solid form of Buck Foreman. She'd caught him with his finger about an inch from the doorbell.

"What's up?" she asked, stepping back.

Foreman came into the house, pulling out his ubiquitous cop's notebook. "I'm back from a quick canvass south of town—that seems to be the direction our subjects took."

Michael got up from the couch. "Motel people recognized Chad's picture?"

Buck nodded. "Several places recognized him as a semiregular customer. Always paid in cash, signing himself in as 'Frank Chambers.'"

"Well, I guess that's better than 'John Smith,'" Liza quipped.

Michael, however, frowned. "Very literary. Frank Chambers is the name of the character who gets into the adulterous affair in *The Postman Always Rings Twice*."

Liza shook her head. "Well, all through school, Chad had his nose in a book." Sometimes he was so busy reading, he didn't even notice trouble—usually in the person of J.J. Pauncecombe—coming at him.

On the other hand . . . "So he actually signed a hotel register as a famous adulterer? That kind of gives away what he wanted the room for."

Buck nodded. "Always the same sort of motel, too. The front desk located some distance from the actual units. One person could check in and the other could pull his or her car right up to the door."

"So the question becomes, who was pulling up?" Michael asked.

"We got lucky there." Buck consulted his notes. "One Jason Katz was working the front desk and had to go and quiet down a loud party in one of the rooms. He was walking past Room 119, registered to Frank Chambers, as a woman exited a car and entered the room. She passed directly under one of the porch lights, and he saw her clearly."

Buck snapped the notebook shut. "It was Brandy Pauncecombe."

"If you could find out that much with only an afternoon's search, I bet anyone could find out a lot more," Liza slowly said. "Could you give me a copy of what you just said? I'm going to a memorial for Chad Redbourne, and I'm sure Sheriff Clements will be in attendance. If I pass this to him, he can pick up the ball from there."

Foreman opened to a new page on his notebook, scribbled away for a moment, then tore out the sheet of paper. "Y'know, you're handing your pal the sheriff a ticking bomb here," he warned. "Redbourne screwing around might offer a personal rather than political motive for his death. But if he's screwing with the wife of the local political boss—well, that becomes a major political issue for a sheriff facing re-election."

"Clements will be annoyed to find me getting involved in the investigation anyway. But . . ." Liza paused, looking up at Buck's stern face in full tough-cop mode. "As a cop, would you rather have a lead on a murder case or not?"

Buck's shoulders sank a little. "I'd rather have it," he admitted.

Liza nodded and started out the door.

But she still heard Buck muttering behind her, "I just hope that Clements doesn't disappoint you."

Freney's Funeral Home stood at the edge of Killamook, doing business in a vaguely colonial-looking building that always reminded Liza of Mount Vernon surrounded by a parking lot.

Maybe Washington didn't sleep here, but he could have been laid out here, that irreverent side of her brain suggested as she pulled into the lot. She found plenty of cars ahead of her, including a couple of police cruisers on traffic duty.

One of the deputies waving her along turned out to be Brenna Ross, who gave her a surprised look.

Liza rolled down her window. "Earning some overtime?" she asked with a grin.

Brenna replied with a grin of her own. "Yeah—thanks for justifying my presence here."

Let's just hope she doesn't have to step in and rescue me from a raging mob, Liza thought, her smile going a bit wry.

She parked and walked in without any other exciting incidents.

Liza had attended enough wakes at Freney's—hell, Ralph Freney had undertaken the undertaking for both Liza's father and her mother. The funeral director had mixed unctuousness with an eye for a buck that would have been right at home in the most cutthroat Hollywood studio.

Tonight, Freney had arranged a funeral extravaganza, guest of honor or not. Usually, the building was divided into three "remembrance rooms," as Freney had explained in his most syrupy tones. But the accordion dividers had been pushed into the walls to create one huge space. Every folding chair in the joint had been pressed into service to create an audience area with three aisles leading to a podium up front.

Most of the chairs were already occupied, but the empty space at the rear of the room, usually occupied by family members exchanging murmured condolences, were filled with political types pressing the flesh.

John Jacob Pauncecombe stood off to the right of the main entrance, looking as if he expected everyone to kiss his ring. He looked older than his pictures in the newspaper—Liza could make out broken blood vessels under the skin of his cheeks and nose. But with his silver hair brushed straight back, he was still handsome, in a fleshy, boozy kind of way.

Beside him stood J.J., looking like a copy of his father that never quite came into focus. The harsh, confident lines of the father's face were blurred in the son's. Instead of his father's ready smile, J.J. seemed more petulant. A wispy blond stood at J.J.'s side, clinging to his arm, a black dress all but washing her out. Liza had heard that the younger Pauncecombe had gotten married, but she'd never seen his wife before.

Then Brandy stepped out from behind the family group. She'd dressed very simply in a long black skirt and black silk blouse, a thin gold chain at her neck, and that damned snake belt advertising her nonexistent waist. Each golden scale must have been faceted—together they gleamed against the dark material of her skirt.

Brandy had wisely eased up on her makeup, but even so her tan and her dramatic skin tone stood out against the somber clothing. In fact, of the Pauncecombe contingent, she made the most vivid impression. The old man was imposing but a bit faded for all his bonhomie. J.J. seemed to try too hard.

Liza shook her head. Leave it to Brandy to steal the show.

She turned away to survey the rest of the crowd and spotted Sheriff Clements standing with his back to the opposite wall. He'd worn his dress uniform with a darker brown, vaguely military-looking tunic and a matching tie.

The sheriff stood quietly observing the throng of

politicos and wannabes busily shaking hands. But Liza
noticed nobody was pressing the flesh with Clements. In
fact, there was a little bubble of open space around the
county's top cop.

*I guess nobody wants to be seen with the sheriff in case
the machine decides to go with another candidate,* Liza
thought.

On the other hand, this avoidance behavior might make
it easier for her to pass along her information. Slipping a
hand in her pocket, she folded the page from Buck's notebook until it fit in her palm. Then she stepped over to Sheriff Clements and shook hands.

He hesitated for a moment as he felt the paper between
their palms.

"And what the heck is this, Ms. Kelly?" he asked in a
low voice.

Liza smiled and nodded as if they were having a desul-
tory conversation. "It's the address of a motel outside the
county and the name of a desk clerk who identified Chad
Redbourne as having an affair . . ." She lowered her voice
a little more. "With Brandy Pauncecombe."

The sheriff's face remained bland, but Liza noticed that
his hand tightened around the piece of paper hers held hidden. He gave her a polite smile, but there was no trace of
humor in his eyes. "And how solid is this information?"

"Buck Foreman dug it up."

Clements nodded. "Well, thank you for this exciting can
of worms you've just opened for me."

"Sheriff, I'm sorry—"

He cut her off with a mild headshake. "We don't want
people to see us standing here talking too long."

With a nod, he stepped away. The bubble of empty space
remained around him as he moved through the crowd. People stepped aside as if even brushing him might pass on
something contagious.

Brandy Pauncecombe left her husband and came over
to Liza. "If things keep going the way they've been, your
friend may not have that gold badge much longer."

Liza had to keep herself from smacking her old rival. "Would that matter much to you?" she asked.

Brandy shrugged, a move she liked to do because it made interesting jiggles on her superstructure. "I like Sheriff Clements—he's like a big ol' bear." Her big dark eyes narrowed in distaste as she took in the mob of office- and favor-seekers around them. "Y'know, you and I were the only ones to say hello to him this evening. The rest of this bunch didn't have the guts."

Liza followed Brandy's gaze to where Oscar Smutz stood fawning over the elder Pauncecombe and J.J.

Brandy shrugged again. "Course, it doesn't much matter whether I have guts or not. Nobody much cares about what I think."

She made her way back to her husband with a carefully calculated amount of hip action, causing a small trail of distraction among the male members of the assemblage.

Look but don't touch, Liza thought.

She found herself a seat on the edge of the last row of chairs—someplace that would allow an easy escape if the speeches became too gag-worthy.

And as the people settled down and the speeches began, it was enough to make a yak retch. As a professional, though, she was fascinated by the wild divergence in tone. It wasn't easy, mixing a eulogy for the deceased's public service while tiptoeing around the notion of murder or suicide and also distancing the powers that be from any connection with whatever got Chad killed. The speechifying sounded almost as schizophrenic as the speakers, all of it glued together and lubricated by the same old political oil.

John Jacob Pauncecombe even had the nerve to quote the line from Shakespeare about the good that men do being interred with their bones.

What he'd like to do is bury all the dirty business Chad did for him and his honest and honorable pals, Liza thought. *Either they'll shove it all under the rug, or they'll pile it on Chad as the conveniently dead scapegoat.*

She watched as Pauncecombe finished to the obligatory

applause. Without a doubt, the situation had turned out well for old John Jacob. He'd disposed of not only a potential political embarrassment but a personal one as well. Chad certainly wouldn't be doing the horizontal mambo with Brandy anymore.

Liza watched the older man's features as he left the podium; not that she expected to see any signs of guilt—or any other honest emotion, for that matter. Politicians were as good as actors at maintaining a pose—maybe even better. Actors could let go of the role once the play ended or the camera stopped. Political types had to keep the mask on whenever they were in public.

Pauncecombe's oration was essentially the grand finale. He stepped off for yet another round of handshakes and backslaps, making a procession down the side of the room. Apparently, the etiquette went back to the days of royalty— or at least Elvis. Nobody else was supposed to exit until the king had left the building.

Things didn't go as usual, though.

For starters, Ralph Freney wanted more than the handshake John Jacob bestowed on him. The funeral director licked his lips, hanging on to the great man's hand, halting him right beside Liza's seat.

"Always a pleasure to put our facilities at your disposal," Freney said in his most syrupy voice. "But I'm afraid there's a problem. The check I was given—it seems there were insufficient funds."

Pauncecombe's face went bright red, bringing the broken blood vessels up into high relief. But it wasn't embarrassment. This was John Jacob's famous temper. Liza had seen it before, twenty years ago when J.J. screwed up—or the school board didn't fall in immediately to cover up the infraction.

As Ava had warned, however, it seemed to be on a hair trigger nowadays. "So you think you had to bring this to my attention?" Pauncecombe barked.

Freney shrank back, faltering, "It's the account—the Party's general fund—"

Pauncecombe cut him off. "Who cut it?"

"Mr. Davis from the committee."

"Well, why the hell didn't you go to him?" John Jacob's bloodshot eyes seared their way across the crowd. Liza noticed a slight disturbance—probably the hapless Davis ducking farther back.

The political boss didn't notice, ranting on. "What do you expect me to do? Pay your bill out of my own pocket? Take it up with Davis." His gaze settled on his son. "And if he still screws up, talk to J.J."

Pauncecombe just about thrust the funeral director away. But even though the ritual butt-kissing resumed immediately, he didn't calm down. He was moody and brusque as the sycophants continued to come up to him. Liza could see the conflicted expressions on the faces of the hangers-on. Which was the worse move? Step up and have their heads bitten off? Or hold back and perhaps be remembered for not being on board?

Liza rose from her seat and trailed behind Pauncecombe's retinue, enjoying the show. Then a sudden eddy in the crowd obstructed the royal progress.

Sheriff Clements stood in the doorway, the magical empty space around him even larger as people shied away, unwilling even to be seen near the political outsider, especially considering Pauncecombe's uncertain frame of mind.

Clements tried to make his approach look natural, reaching out to shake hands with the boss. From the tight lines on his face, though, the sheriff might just as well have been offering his arm to a hungry mountain lion.

"We need a private meeting." Clements's voice was quiet, but it penetrated the sudden, surprised hush his unexpected approach had created. "I have some questions—"

"Questions?" Pauncecombe's response seemed several decibels louder. "You've got questions? For me?"

The sheriff stood his ground. "Regarding the Redbourne case, we need to eliminate—"

"You'd better watch your mouth, Clements," the Party

chief interrupted. "You're not so secure in your job that *you* can't be eliminated."

Pauncecombe pushed out of the room, his favorites rushing after him.

Bert Clements stood stone-faced. He definitely did *not* fall into that category.

Arriving home, Liza tried to lose herself in work; not that the results were all that good. The events at the memorial had disconcerted her—especially the way the political cognoscenti seemed to think that the sheriff's job was hanging by a thread.

Now she worried over what she and her scrap of paper had done. *If Bert Clements loses his job, it's not as if he has lots of places to go,* Liza fretted. *He won't just get bucked down to chief investigator. Not with Oscar Smutz in charge.* She sighed. *Not with a vengeful political leadership after him.*

Michael finally waved a hand between her face and the computer screen, saying, "Let's put on the late news."

Liza didn't want to watch. He just about had to carry her over to the couch, eliciting some excited barks from Rusty.

It wasn't as bad as she'd expected. There were no lurid reports about a rift between the head of Killamook's law enforcement and the head of the county's political machine. By the time John Jacob Pauncecombe had emerged from Freney's Funeral Home and into the view of the various camera crews, he'd regained control of himself. His somber, unsmiling face seemed in keeping with the serious affair he was leaving.

The only other bad moment came when Oscar Smutz's fat face appeared on the screen later in the newscast. The daylight background reassured Liza slightly—this hadn't been shot at the memorial.

But as Smutz continued to second-guess the sheriff's investigation, Liza's unease grew. In the eyes of the media—and thus, of the public—Oscar had moved from glorified gadfly to the position of insurgent candidate. And after this evening's disaster, he'd also have the backing of the Killamook machine.

The news ended, and one of the network late-night comedy shows came on. Liza reached for the remote, but Michael took it. "Leave it on," he said. "You look as if you could use some cheering up."

Unfortunately, listening to the monologue seemed to have the opposite effect. Either the writers were really having an off day, or Liza's mood was so foul, nothing could change it. She watched in apathy as the host promised a new segment after the commercials.

The show returned with a montage of clips featuring famous political and entertainment types and a spinning logo that resolved itself into the words FACES IN THE NEWS.

The host appeared behind his desk, saying, "You know, there are always public affairs shows on Sunday morning, but the people they have on are already famous. We think it's better to introduce you to faces *before* they get famous. For instance, here's somebody involved in a political race up in Oregon . . ."

Liza gasped as Oscar Smutz's face filled the screen.

It had to come from one of yesterday's TV interviews. The sound wasn't on, but he was certainly running his mouth. The image froze in the middle of a distinctive mannerism Liza had noticed. Whenever Smutz had something particularly damaging to say, he took a deep breath, his cheeks swelling and his eyes popping.

"And here's a way to remember him," the host said as the clip went on, this time with sound.

"What this county needs in a sheriff," Smutz began, then took a deep breath. But the studio engineers had made an addition to the tape—the loud call of a bullfrog. As Oscar's face swelled up on the screen, it was accompanied by a deep-voiced "Ribbit!"

"Is a trained individual who understands the local

situation," Smutz went on, then the inhale clip came on again. "Ribbit!"

"And can think on the fly." The pop-eyed face appeared twice more. "Ribbit! Ribbit!"

Liza's mouth hung open, and her eyes had probably popped as wide as Oscar's. Michael, however, joined the studio audience in laughing hysterically. "That is priceless."

But Liza shook her head. "No, that's very expensive," she said. "Or it should be. Unless I miss my guess, this is the work of Michelle Markson."

11

Liza jumped to her feet and ran to the kitchen and its phone. She pressed one of the buttons preprogrammed with Michelle's cell number.

Michelle answered on the third ring. "Yes?"

Liza heard familiar background noise—at least, familiar for Michelle come evening. Somebody was playing piano lounge-style, glassware clinked, slightly boozy voices talked and laughed. Somehow, somewhere, whenever Michelle left the office, she moved on to a party.

"Michelle, Liza Kelly here."

Before Liza could go on, Michelle interrupted. "So my caller ID tells me. It doesn't tell me why you're calling at this hour."

"Michelle, *liebchen*," a petulant, somewhat accented voice came from the background. "Why do you go away again? We were going to dance, I thought."

"Bruno, I have told you once already not to disturb me while I am on the phone."

Liza allowed herself a smile. This guy had just one strike left.

Grumbling noises moved off—presumably a rebuffed Bruno.

"I want to know how you managed the bit I just saw on late-night TV," Liza said. "The one starring the loathsome face of Oscar Smutz."

"That toad who's been going around suggesting that you committed murder?" Michelle asked.

"The magic of television made him look—and sound— more like a frog."

"Why, I don't know what you're talking about," Michelle said virtuously but with a laugh in her voice.

"If you go after every bozo who passes a remark about a client, you won't have much time to be going to parties," Liza said.

"I only do this for friends," Michelle told her. "I have so few, you see, it takes up hardly any of my time at all."

Her voice returned to its usual acid tone as she said, "I sincerely hope you've accomplished something to make the effort worth my while."

Liza relayed what Buck had discovered.

"Well, that's certainly a different sort of motive. And it would seem to narrow down the range of suspects to the aggrieved husband, wouldn't it?"

"He's got a temper that hasn't improved with age," Liza admitted. "I wonder if he's spry enough to string up the corpse the way he did."

She sighed. "Given the way things are with the sheriff, I don't think I'll be hearing much about the investigation."

"But don't you have another friend with the police?" Michelle asked. "That sergeant person?"

"It wouldn't hurt to talk to Ted," Liza said slowly. "I'll give him a call."

She glanced back to the living room, where Michael still sat watching the late-night host doing an interview with a starlet in a very abbreviated dress.

Well, he looks distracted, she thought, punching in the number for Ted Everard's cell phone.

*   *   *

They had agreed to meet for lunch in downtown Killamook, so the next day Liza drove over to the county seat.
She parked a couple of blocks off Broad Street and then
strolled along, taking in the ever-changing display of tourists being separated from their surplus cash. It wasn't taw-
dry, just aggressively quaint.

Liza saw Ted drive past in his government-issue grinder
and waved. With a policeman's luck, he pulled into a parking spot on the main drag.

After a quick kiss, he said, "As part of my interrogation
of the elections staff, I asked for a decent place where real
people ate, not sightseers. It's supposed to be up two blocks
and across . . ."

His voice was drowned out by patriotic music as a pickup
truck done up in red, white, and blue bunting came down
the street, rolling to a stop on the block ahead of them.

Oscar Smutz came out of the cab, carrying a plastic
milk carton to give himself a boost onto the bed of the
truck. He had a bullhorn in one hand, which he quickly
raised to his face as he launched into what sounded like a
practiced spiel.

"The name is Smutz, Oscar Smutz, and I'm running for
sheriff of Killamook County." As he spoke, a crowd began
gathering on the sidewalk.

Oscar took a deep breath, inflating his face just as he had
on TV the night before. "It's time to bring some decency to
the way the law is enforced in this county. The incumbent
is actually preparing to launch a purely political investigation into the private life of one of our most upstanding
citizens. And why? To confuse the issue over the slipshod
way he's running a major murder case."

Oscar took another deep breath—and as he did, someone yelled "Ribbit!" from the back of the crowd.

That got a laugh, throwing the candidate off. He vamped
for a moment, saying, "Voters of Killamook County!" into

his bullhorn as he tried to pick up the thread of his speech. "Don't you want a sheriff who'll enforce the law, not act as if he's above it?"

He took another deep breath, and now three voices yelled, "Ribbit!" from the crowd.

Oscar's face went brick red as he glared into the crowd. "Under my administration, the Sheriff's Department will rejoin its proper partnership with the county government."

"Dividing the spoils," Ted muttered under his breath.

"Instead of launching senseless vendettas to cover up the failings at the top," Smutz continued.

Unfortunately, he had to take a breath again, and half the crowed responded with, "Ribbit!"

Smutz glared around in impotent fury.

"I guess it's kind of hard to convince people about what a take-charge administrator you are when you can't even control the folks at your own pep rally," Liza said.

"And just to make it worse . . ." Ted nodded to the other side of the crowd, where Murph stood with a micro-cassette recorder, keeping track of this whole debacle for the *Oregon Daily*.

Some of the color drained from Smutz's face when he saw that, but it came back to near stroke level when he spotted Liza on the outskirts of the crowd, too.

"Voters!" he blared into the loudspeaker. "It'll take more than cheap shots to silence honest criticism. It's bad enough that Clements is using his California connections to try and smear me. What's worse is that one of his Hollywood pals should be a suspect! She was right there with the body!"

He sucked in another breath, but whatever he was going to say was lost as just about the whole crowd joined in a chant of "Ribbit! Ribbit! Ribbit!"

Smutz got so angry, he threw down the bullhorn, which promptly bounced out of the truck bed and onto the pavement. He had to scramble ingloriously after it, then jumped into the cab of the pickup and screeched off, leaving his milk crate behind.

As the crowd broke up, Liza and Ted found themselves behind a tourist couple.

"That was hilarious," the male half of the couple said. "They actually got that guy from TV to come here and act like he was running for office."

"Yeah," the female tourist agreed. "That's a lot better than all this old-fashioned stuff they've got around here."

Ted glanced at Liza, trying to keep a straight face. "The people have spoken," he said in a low voice.

The outside of the restaurant Ted led them to had the same sort of artificial retro look dominating the rest of Broad Street. But it had a rear terrace with tables shaded by umbrellas, and real people—locals, not visitors—enjoying lunch.

The menu looked pretty interesting, too. Liza had a four-cheese panini with tomato and grilled sweet onions while Ted went for the chicken salad platter.

"You've got to learn to live a little," Liza told him, tilting her head to keep a string of cheese from landing on her chin.

"I lived already this week with fried chicken out of the bucket," he replied, raising a forkful to his mouth. "Nice—and fresh."

"With hints of earth tones, chocolate, and blueberry?" Liza suggested, mocking the extravagance that usually accompanied wine reviews.

"No, but I think some chopped tarragon and maybe a little lemon went into this."

He put the fork down. "That was some curve you threw at Bert Clements."

Liza paused in mid-bite. "It's not like I wanted to." She explained about the help that Michelle had sent up from L.A., hearing Kevin's story, and Buck's subsequently nailing it down. "What were we supposed to do then? *Not* tell Clements?"

Ted poked at his salad. "Well, it certainly concentrates the spotlight on the old man."

Liza nodded. It turned John Jacob Pauncecombe into

that staple figure of domestic comedy—and tragedy—the cuckolded husband.

"Clements started asking questions almost as soon as I passed along what Buck found," she said. "Did he have anything else to make him suspect Pauncecombe?"

"And here I thought we were just having a nice, friendly luncheon." Ted settled back in his seat with a sarcastic look. "Discussing the investigation is a no-no. Especially since, technically speaking, you're still a suspect."

"Oh, come on," Liza burst out. "I didn't do it, and you know I didn't."

Ted shrugged. "I'll tell you what we think happened—if you know any better, feel free to correct us. There's no sign of a struggle, so we think the murder took place on that nice open terrace."

Liza nodded. "Strangle Chad, dump him in the wheelbarrow, and trundle him off to the folly. That suggests a certain familiarity with the house, knowing where to find the wheelbarrow, the folly—and some rope." She shuddered. "Hoisting him up must have been a problem—dealing with all that deadweight."

"That was actually handled pretty well," Ted told her. "Two loops on either end of the rope. One goes around Chad's neck. The other fits the killer's foot. Redbourne wasn't the biggest guy in the world. Even your body weight would have been enough to pull him up."

Liza gave him a look. "Thanks a lot for the weight comment. And do I have to remind you that I'm trying to get *off* the suspect list, not on?"

He just went on with his description. "The inside of that beehive thing is all rough stone. Snag the other loop on one of those projecting bits of rock, and the job is done."

Liza chewed that over, along with a bite of her sandwich. "And there was nothing inside the house?"

"No confessions, suicide notes, or incriminating photos." Ted shrugged. "For a bachelor establishment, it was remarkably orderly."

"Chad was always a good boy," Liza said. "He probably had the neatest locker in Killamook High."

Ted leaned back in his seat, watching her. "Yeah, everything was squared away, until we got to his underwear drawer. Half the whiteys were tidy, the rest were all crumpled in. We found the same thing with his socks and shirts. What does that tell you?"

"He changed cleaning ladies?" Liza suggested.

That earned her an exasperated look from Ted. "Maybe if I add that his suitcase was tossed on top of his shoes, instead of taking its usual place in the back of his bedroom closet . . ."

"Shirts, underwear, socks—he'd packed a bag."

Ted nodded. "That got hurriedly—and messily—unpacked."

Liza took another bite of her sandwich for mental fortification. "You said Chad was pretty rattled during your meeting with him. Maybe he saw the handwriting on the wall for the whole ghost voter scam and decided to get out of town."

"And then changed his mind?" Ted asked.

"Maybe more like a change of plan," Liza said, "if the killer found the bags afterward."

She shook her head. "However you look at the motive—political or personal—Chad's leaving town would have solved the problem."

"He wouldn't be sinning anymore," Ted said. "But an angry husband might have still been ticked off over past transgressions."

Liza shook her head, feeling a little sad. "Whatever the motive, the killer apparently didn't know that Chad was leaving, found him on the terrace, did the deed—and discovered it wasn't necessary."

"In fact, the packed bag screwed up the carefully staged suicide out in the folly," Ted added.

"So the bag gets hastily unpacked," Liza said. "But haste makes mess."

Ted smiled. "At least inside the dresser."

Liza smiled back. "Weaving the tangled web and all

that stuff. I guess that's what happens when you kill first
and ask questions later."

Ted attacked his salad for a few minutes in silence, his
smile slowly fading. "All of that seems to fit the facts. But
it leaves one question niggling at me."

Liza paused in the midst of dabbing her lips with a nap-
kin. "What's that?"

"The cause of death—he was garroted." Ted pushed
away his plate. "That means Redbourne had to turn his
back on his killer. I don't see that happening in the middle
of a big confrontation—"

"Like if John Jacob Pauncecombe came to accuse Chad
of sleeping with Brandy . . ." Liza paused. "I could see the
old man strangling Chad." In fact, her mind's eye could
easily conjure up an image of the older man's big hands
closing around Chad's throat.

She went on more slowly. "Maybe I could see Chad
not wanting to meet the other guy's eyes. But you'd think
he'd have to notice Pauncecombe picking up the wire or
whatever he used to do the job." She frowned. "We've been
going on the notion that this was a sort of spur-of-the-
moment thing—that the killer was improvising."

"Unless," Ted said, "it was a carefully planned killing that
went off the rails. The killer sneaks up on Redbourne—no
talk, no questions, just choking him with a garrote brought
for the purpose. The fake suicide could have been planned
in advance. And then the packed suitcase turns up."

"If it were planned, Pauncecombe wouldn't start hol-
lering at being questioned," Liza objected. "He'd have his
alibi established and all ready to recite."

"Unless it's not Pauncecombe."

"Then I gave Clements a bum steer that only led him
into trouble." All of a sudden, Liza's lunch wasn't sitting all
that well. "We must be missing something."

"Like more facts or some solid evidence like the murder
weapon." Ted pushed his chair back. "Well, I can't spend
all day constructing elaborate theories with you. I have an
investigation to pursue at the county elections office."

"How is that going?" Liza asked.

Ted made a face. "All of the staffers—shall I say the surviving staffers?—seem to be glorified file clerks, paper pushers. Whatever Redbourne was doing with the phantom voters, he didn't seem to let anyone in on it. We may wind up having to go weeding through every voter in the county."

"Sounds like a lot of time and expense," Liza said.

"Tell me about it," Ted replied gloomily. "Well, off to the salt mines."

They paid their bill and headed back out to Broad Street. Liza waved good-bye as Ted drove off.

Whistling tunelessly, she started up the street.

Speaking of the salt mines, I guess I'd better get back home and work on some sudokus, she thought.

Retracing the route to her car took her past the offices of Killamook County Trust, one of the bigger local banks. A large poster in the window featured a dog at a computer, touting the ease of automated banking.

That's all I'd need, Rusty able to go online and withdraw funds for doggie treats, Liza thought.

But just as she was about to turn away, she spotted a familiar face—in fact, a pair of them. J.J. Pauncecombe and Oscar Smutz sat in front of the manager's desk.

Liza remembered that bit of byplay at Chad's memorial the evening before, where the undertaker had complained that the check for the event hadn't cleared. She sidestepped behind the dog poster and peered around it.

The bank manager looked concerned as he consulted some papers in front of him. When he was done, J.J. got up without a word and headed for the door.

Liza quickly got out of the way. The last time she'd seen J.J. look that way had been at the championship game when J.J. had his gong rung pretty hard by a big linebacker. The coach had pulled J.J. out of the game, but for half an hour, he'd just sat on the bench, his eyes seeing nothing, his face sagging.

12

Liza waited until she got to her car before taking out her cell phone and calling Ava Barnes.

"Is this a call to tell me how many more columns you're about to e-mail in, or do you have something exciting to pass along about this Redbourne mess?" That was Ava, always the editor.

"I went to the memorial for Chad last evening," Liza said.

"They actually barred Murph at the door," Ava told her. "He was getting ready to slug somebody until he realized there were TV cameras around."

"He didn't want to make a spectacle of himself in front of the enemy?"

"The competition," Ava corrected. "I understand he missed one bit of excitement. The sheriff tried to ask John Jacob Pondscum some questions and got his head bitten off for his trouble."

"Ah." Of course that story would be making the rounds immediately. "I saw some of that exchange," Liza admitted. "Any other fallout from it?"

"No," Ava replied. "Not yet."

That didn't make Liza feel much better. But she had another subject to discuss with her editor.

"Something else happened," she said. "At the end of the memorial, Mr. Freney came up to John Jacob. He said the check that the committee had cut to pay him had insufficient funds."

"They must be yanking Freney's chain." Ava sounded very certain. "I've never heard of the Party hurting for money."

"Where do John Jacob and the boys do their banking?" Liza asked.

"Oh, they spread their loot around to most every bank in the county," Ava replied, "five, maybe six banks. Probably more goes to the local operations like Killamook Trust than the branches of the bigger outfits. Our political friends figure they can exert more leverage on neighbors who might need a favor instead of a manager who answers to a head office somewhere out of their control."

"Well, I just walked past Killamook Trust," Liza told her friend. "J.J. Pauncecombe was sitting at a desk with Oscar Smutz. And they looked as if they were getting an earful of bad news."

"We don't have a financial reporter at this office." Ava spoke slowly but quickly made up her mind. "I can send Murph around to ask some questions, though. He knows enough people in the various offices."

"And if they don't give him a straight answer, he can probably figure out what they're hiding," Liza added.

Now it was her turn to hesitate. "Last night was the first time I saw J.J. in I don't know how many years. He got married, I see."

"Yeah, he picked up Donna the Doormat as some sort of consolation prize while he was flunking out of law school in Portland." Ava definitely did not sound complimentary. "I guess you could call her the Queen of Denial, considering the way she shuts her eyes while he cats around."

"So what exactly is J.J.'s place in the machine's pecking order?" Liza asked. "I saw him standing right beside his dad, and when Freney came up with this check problem, John Jacob referred him to J.J."

"That seems to be the kind of job he gets nowadays—responsibility without much authority," Ava said. "Our boy J.J. suffers from a bad case of Prince Charles Syndrome—he's the heir apparent, but when the hell is he supposed to inherit?"

"Huh." Liza let her breath out in a puff. "Makes me wonder whether J.J. was at the bank on his dad's say-so, or if he's looking into it on his own hook. Then, too, why was Oscar Smutz along for the ride?"

"Well, the guy was a cop," Ava pointed out.

"So what do you think? Does that make him the closest thing the machine has to an in-house investigator? And if so, what are they investigating?"

"I guess that's what Murph will have to find out." From the sound of Ava's voice, she intended to call her investigative ace to get on the story right away.

But first, Liza reverted to managing editor mode. "Good-bye," she told Liza. "Go home. Work."

"Yes'm." Liza cut the connection and started her car.

As she drove back to Maiden's Bay, Liza tried to organize what she'd seen and heard over the past few days into some sort of coherent framework. Regrettably, she ended up forced to agree with Ted Everard. Despite all the stuff they had, they didn't know enough.

This case felt like a sudoku puzzle with only a few spaces filled in and no candidates listed in the blanks. To paraphrase the great Donald Rumsfeld, they didn't even have enough to know what they didn't know.

The way this thing had twisted and turned, Liza wasn't all that hot to bring Chad Redbourne's killer to justice. Such high-flown pursuits were more in the way of intellectual skywriting. What mattered more right now was that a live friend was in trouble. Bert Clements had put himself on the Killamook machine's S-list because of a clue that Liza had given him.

And Ava was right—John Jacob Pauncecombe's threats were just the first shoe falling.

Liza stabbed a finger at her car radio. She didn't want to listen, but she figured she'd most likely hear about the machine's next move through their official propaganda arm, KMUC.

The afternoon pundit gassed for a while about national politics; then he announced a guest, the local district attorney, Cy Langdon.

"Here it comes," Liza muttered.

She had no idea as to how successful the DA was at prosecuting and convicting criminals. But even her mom, who barely talked about politics, had Langdon pegged as a stooge for John Jacob Pondscum.

Langdon alternated between folksy language and lawyer-speak, but his meaning was crystal clear. His office was considering legal action against the TV network and the late-night show that had run the clip of Oscar Smutz. Apparently the theory was that they were stifling free speech by holding Oscar up to ridicule.

The subtext was also pretty apparent—that Bert Clements for his own dastardly purposes had pulled a dirty campaign trick.

"It comes down to this." Langdon's voice would have sounded a lot more sincere if he didn't have a slight wheeze. "Do we want outsiders deciding our elections? Or shouldn't the voters of Killamook be free to make up their own minds?"

That steaming shovelful got Liza so annoyed, she switched to the country-western station for the rest of the drive home.

Things were pretty calm back on Hackleberry Drive. Michael had taken Rusty for a walk, picked up some provisions, and copyedited some of Liza's rough columns.

He also had a message from Buck and Alvin, asking for a meeting ASAP.

They convened over at Mrs. Halvorsen's house. She gave everyone thimble-sized glasses of sherry. Then Liza went over everything she'd learned from Ted Everard about the sheriff's investigation and added what she'd seen at the offices of Killamook Trust.

"I talked to Ava Barnes about that, too," she finished. "She's putting a good reporter onto checking with the banks around here."

"I have some connections in the banking business," Buck offered. "Let me talk to them and have them ask around."

"I can do that, too," Alvin said.

"The next item, from my point of view, is what can we do to help the sheriff? Ava thinks it's just a matter of time before the machine comes up with something unpleasant. Pauncecombe certainly threatened his job because of something we dug up."

"I don't know how much more you can do," Buck pointed out. "Technically, you're still a suspect."

"Not to mention that the people you want to protect the sheriff from are using you as a political football," Alvin added.

"And even though I know that you, Mr. Foreman, and Mr. Hunzinger mean well, other people don't," Mrs. H. put in. "The district attorney was on the radio today, talking about outsiders tampering with the election."

"I heard that," Liza said gloomily.

"It's just that whatever you do could be taken the wrong way." The older woman looked at her watch. "The evening news is coming on."

She turned on the big, old television set in front of the couch. They started with pretty much the same local fare—a breaking story about a fire burning up stores in Pacific City, followed by an interview with a food bank activist in Nehalem.

Next came some stories relating to national news, and then the anchor team went into "happy talk" mode.

"A local political candidate got some national coverage last night," the male anchor said with a smile.

"But it's not the kind of attention he might want," his female counterpart went on. "Here's Pat McNabb with the story."

The now-infamous film clip of Oscar Smutz looking

like a bullfrog ran, segueing into locally shot footage of the candidate on his pickup truck. It wasn't the same speech-making try that Liza and Ted had seen, but it ended the same way, with chants of "Ribbit" drowning Smutz out.

Liza shrugged. "Well, I guess the cameras had to catch it sooner or later."

The scene shifted back to the newsroom and the anchors. "In more Killamook political news, Orem Whelan became the acting elections chief, filling the office of the recently deceased Chad Redbourne. Given the murky circumstances of his predecessor's demise, Whelan is promoting tough new standards."

A film clip came on, featuring a rabbity-looking man trying to seem stern. "It seems there is only one way to ensure there are no irregularities in this election cycle," he said, reading from a prepared statement. "I am requiring a new set of nominating petitions from each candidate."

"There's the other shoe," Liza remarked. "The machine has the manpower to go out and get new petitions signed with no problem. But independent candidates like Ray Massini—and now Sheriff Clements—will have problems."

Michael nodded. "Very neat. Takes care of two birds with one stone."

"And we can expect this stooge to go over their petitions with a microscope to invalidate any signatures they can."

"But that—that's not right," Mrs. Halvorsen huffed. "They want to keep us from voting for the mayor and the sheriff?"

"If this works, they might not even be able to run," Alvin explained. "Although I suppose the whole matter could wind up in court."

"Where the Killamook machine will keep delaying things until the election is over."

"We can't allow that," Mrs. H. said decisively.

"I don't know that there's much that you or I can do." Liza gestured to the others in the room. "And three of us aren't even registered to vote around here."

"Well, I'm going to start calling all my friends—and I have a lot of them." Mrs. Halvorsen got up. "Some of them agreed to help when you were running . . ." She broke off with an embarrassed smile at Liza. "When we thought you were running for mayor. And after they hear about this dirty trick, I'll bet I can get a lot more."

She turned to Alvin. "You're a lawyer. What do we need to put on these petitions? Do we have to file papers?"

His round face looked befuddled as he blinked up at her from his seat on the couch. "I'm a criminal lawyer," he began. "I don't know—"

"Well, can't you get on Google or something and find out? We need to be ready to start tomorrow morning." The older woman softened her tone slightly as she asked Liza, "Dear, could we use your computer to do the research and print things out?"

"Um," Liza replied, feeling almost as befuddled as Alvin at this sudden whirlwind of political energy. "Sure."

So, instead of working at her computer, Liza spent the evening constructing some sudoku by hand while Alvin did research and then Michael printed out the necessary forms and created a few dozen blank petitions.

"These will be used for originals," he explained to Liza. "Mrs. H. has people going to all the copy shops in the county. She's really burning up the phone lines."

"What has she got Buck doing?" Liza asked with a grin. "Licking envelopes?"

"No, he's making up the lists of who's doing what. Mrs. H. gave his cell phone as the callback number. Apparently she's got all these calling trees for church events, prayers—"

"Gossip," Liza put in.

"Anyway, when she put her mind to it, she was able to recruit a pretty impressive volunteer organization."

"Now all they need is a name," Liza joked.

"How about Killamook Freed from Corruption?" Michael suggested.

"KFC—very funny." Liza paused for a second. "I think

it should be something like the League of Little Old Ladies."

"If you use the preposition, you'd get LoLOL for an acronym," Michael said. "Isn't that computer-speak for Laugh Out Loud?"

"By the time Mrs. H. gets done with them, the Killamook machine will be laughing out of the other side of their mouths," Liza predicted.

By ten o'clock, the storm of political activity died down. Nominating petitions for both Ray Massini and Bert Clements stood ready for reproduction, Mrs. H. had given the marching orders for the next morning, and she and her troops had hit the hay in preparation for a strenuous day of campaigning.

Michael asked Liza if he could turn on the television. "There's a mystery series my agent wants me to keep an eye on—I'm not sure whether he's hoping to get me a scripting gig or a novelization."

Liza didn't pay much attention. The plot had holes, the dialogue was pretty silly, and anyway, she was deep in sudoku-land.

After checking out her latest effort, she made a clean copy.

By the time she'd finished, the late news had come on. This was a Portland station, but they had picked up footage of Oscar Smutz being ribbeted into silence on the campaign trail. They also had Orem Whelan talking about the new tack by the elections commission, and then for good measure threw in Cy Langdon and his complaints about outsiders.

"Big news day for Killamook," Michael commented.

"I guess that's their idea of balanced coverage." Liza slumped on the sofa, frowning at the screen.

Michael put an arm around her shoulders. "However this goes, Liza, we're in it together."

"You don't think this is going to turn out well?" she asked in a small voice.

"I don't know," Michael admitted. "We've got two

7	3		2		8		9	5
1			6		9			2
				7				
9	4						2	1
		1				4		
8	6						7	9
			9					
2			8		3			6
3	1		4		2		5	7

high-powered criminal and investigative types next door, and the best thing they've been able to come up with is a petition drive. We're short on information, and given the political climate around here, we don't seem likely to get any."

" 'A riddle wrapped in an enigma,' " Liza quoted. "Who said that?"

"Churchill, about the Soviets." Michael gave her a rueful smile. "But they don't seem to hold a candle to your Killamook machine. This doesn't seem to be just about personal secrets like your other cases. You've got a whole bunch of people with a vested interest in not letting information get out. And without that—"

"Without that, some good people are going to get hurt." Liza ignored the sportscaster's chatty comments, looking up at Michael.

"Sometimes that's life," he told her. "Bad things happen to good people."

They sat in silence for a while as the news ended and

this network's late-night show came on. This was the big competitor to the show they'd caught last night.

Liza just about zoned out through the monologue until she heard, "Well, things are heating up in the election campaign up in Killamook County, Oregon."

The host paused to give the audience his patented inane smile.

"How's that?" his sidekick inquired from off-camera.

"I suppose you've seen in the news how one candidate ended up looking like a bullfrog," the host went on.

"Ohmigod," Liza muttered. "That went national?"

"It seems this has stirred up a storm of protest—from PETA. They feel it's not ethical to involve another animal in the political process."

"Yeah," the sidekick cracked, "they should stick with elephants and jackasses."

What I want to know is what animals the head writers on these shows were cavorting with—and how Michelle got hold of pictures, Liza thought.

Michael was apparently thinking the same thought. "That woman is scary."

"Anyway, that's the news from Killamook County. Killamook," the host repeated the name as if he were tasting each syllable.

Of course, the audience roared.

13

When Liza came downstairs the next morning, she found that Michael had vacated the couch—in fact, he'd vacated the house. Instead of the husband and bedding she'd expected, Rusty lay in the middle of the couch.

He arched his back and stretched his jaws in a big yawn when he saw her.

"Sure," she said to the dog, "spread your dander right where Michael will put his head."

She evicted Rusty from his place, got a leash on him, and took him for a walk.

When they returned, she fed the dog. Then, leaving Rusty in the kitchen, she sat at her computer and input the sudoku stuff she'd done by hand the night before. After all, she had to inflate her column's cushion. And God only knew what demands Mrs. H. and her newborn campaign might be making on her computer later in the day.

The combination of those thoughts sent Liza to the telephone to call Ava Barnes. Part of it was her publicist background—Mrs. Halvorsen deserved to get some ink for her efforts, and Ava was sure to consider it an interesting story.

But Liza had another reason. "So how is Murph coming along with the banks?" she asked as soon as she finished discussing the nominating petition campaign conducted by the little old ladies.

"So far, all Murph has gotten had been a general round of 'No comments,'" Ava replied. "For some perverse reason, that encourages him. He's convinced that they wouldn't be stonewalling him unless there was a big story behind it."

"How does he figure that?"

Ava smiled. "If they had nothing to hide, somebody would have talked to him. In addition, a few of those somebodies got nervous when he started asking questions."

"Well, I hope he gets a Pulitzer, so long as he finds out what's going on," Liza said.

"Bite your tongue," Ava reproved her. "If Murph got a Pulitzer, he'd be working in Portland—or even worse, New York."

"Have it your way," Liza told her. "By the by, I also asked Buck Foreman and Alvin Hunzinger to work some of their contacts."

"I expect you to share if you hear anything interesting," Ava said. "Remember, you're part of this newspaper, too."

"You'll get the exclusive," Liza promised.

"Good," Ava replied. "I expect we're going to need it."

An excited voice in the background interrupted their conversation.

"Gotta go," Ava growled. "Another fire to put out." She hesitated a second before hanging up. "When you get a chance, I'd like to hear what you think of today's rag."

With that, she cut the connection.

Liza replaced her phone's receiver just as Michael appeared, knocking at the kitchen door.

"I volunteered your car to ferry some of Mrs. H.'s minions," he explained when Liza opened the door. "Whatever she told them, she sure as hell got a lot of people pretty fired up. One of the ladies in my car has a husband who does some Party work—mainly canvassing neighborhoods with nominating petitions."

"And?" Liza asked.

"Well, hubby's not going forth for the boys from Killamook this time around—unless he wants to do without cooked meals." He waggled his eyebrows. "Not to mention other considerations."

Liza made a face. "Ewwwww."

Michael got more serious. "I have to say, I was impressed by those old folks going out there to do battle for what they considered the right thing." He gave her a rueful look. "Maybe you and I have gotten a little jaded, living down in La-La Land."

She cocked her had and grinned at him. "Maybe we have."

He held out a paper sack. "Anyhow, since I was downtown, I stopped off at the bakery and picked up some fresh sweet rolls. Got the newspaper, too."

Liza reached for the *Oregon Daily*. "Ava told me there was something to see in there."

Opening the newspaper on the kitchen table, Liza began paging through. She found what she was looking for in the center spread. Instead of the several editorials the paper usually ran, one long piece stretched the length of the column.

The headline told it all: ARE INSIDERS BETTER?

> *Killamook District Attorney Cyrus Langdon has recently taken several opportunities to express his concern over the satirical portrayal of a local electoral candidate on national television. As he put it, "Outsiders shouldn't decide our elections."*
>
> *The* Oregon Daily *agrees. In our opinion, however, neither should political insiders.*

The piece went on to chronicle all the members of the Killamook machine who had gotten caught with their hands in the cookie jar over the past twenty years. The charges ranged from bid rigging, to sweetheart deals, to out-and-out solicitation of bribes and extortion.

These are just the small fry, the editorial ended, *the occasional fish netted out of many, many more in the sea—or in this case, in a corrupt political ring that has operated for a generation in Killamook. If we want an election to mean anything in this county, we have to go after the big fish and make sure they become true insiders—preferably in the state penal system.*

Liza shook her head and let her breath out in an audible "Whew!" Then she glanced up at Michael, who stood reading over her shoulder.

"Well," she said, "I guess that tears it. We're officially at war."

Rising from the kitchen chair where she'd sat down, Liza went into living room and to her computer. She inserted a CD and started copying files onto it.

Michael trailed after her. "What are you doing?"

"I was going to e-mail some files over to Ava." Liza hit a button, ejected the disc, and put it in a case. "But I think I'll deliver them by hand instead."

The satellite office of the *Oregon Daily* always had a sort of space-age tinge, as if she'd need a ticket on the space shuttle to commute to work. Reality, unfortunately, was definitely a lot more earthbound, even drab. The newspaper had office space on the second floor of a strip mall on the edge of Maiden's Bay.

If the boys in Killamook had their way, this office would probably be outside the county altogether, Liza thought with an ironic smile as she pulled into the sparsely filled parking lot.

The office was only a short drive from Liza's house but a bit of a trudge up a fairly steep set of outdoor stairs to the unmarked metal door above. Liza needed a sharp tug to get the door open, and then she stepped into the reception area—not that you could hold much of a reception in a space barely large enough for a couple of plastic chairs.

The newspaper's logo had recently been added to the wall over the Plexiglas window where Janey Brezinski seemed more harried than usual as she fielded incoming calls.

"Hey, Liza," Janey said, putting a hand over the pickup on her earpiece. "Just a sec."

Liza had already noticed that the inner entrance door, which usually stood propped open, was closed. Janey had to buzz her in.

Looks as if security is on high alert. She had to hide a smile as she walked down the hallway. What were they expecting? A commando attack from Oscar Smutz with an AK-47?

The bull-pen area where the local reporters worked up their stories had several empty desks. No Murph. Liza had hoped to buttonhole him and get a little more on how his story was going. If he told her which of the bankers had been nervous, maybe she could sic Buck and Alvin's friends on them.

Continuing on, she came to the plate glass walls of Ava's office. Ava forestalled Liza's knock on the doorframe with an upheld finger while she spoke on the phone.

"So what brings you here?" she asked as she hung up. "I hope it's not a cash advance. That was another advertiser canceling a spread."

"A lot of that going on after that editorial you published?"

Ava grimaced. "Enough. I also got harangued by John Jacob Pondscum and lectured by Cy Langdon on twisting his words and, quote, 'misrepresenting the actions of a few bad apples in the country administration over a period of decades.' "

"They really should have that engraved in stone over the entrance to the county center," Liza quipped. But she looked at her best friend with concern. "Are you sure this was a good idea, Ava? If this doesn't pan out, it may cost you your job."

"It's a little late to second-guess myself now," Ava replied with a shrug, then grinned. "I'll tell you this, though. We haven't sold this many papers since Obama got sworn in. I'm actually thinking of going back for another press run."

"Will that make up for the ads you're losing?"

"Not hardly," Ava admitted.

"I liked the execution," Liza said. "Instead of coming out for Massini and Clements, you slammed the whole Killamook machine."

"Well, so far neither of them has come out on the record about the editorial." Ava pursed her lips. "Liza, we've been tiptoeing around this mess for years. I thought it was long past time for some plain talk on the subject." A hint of a smile crept over her face. "Do you know how long I've had that list of scuzzballs ready to go into an editorial?"

"You probably compiled it about a week after you came back here," Liza said sweetly. "Oh, by the way." She dug the CD out of her shoulder back and handed it over.

"What's this?" Ava asked.

"A little padding for my pillow," Liza replied. "I figured I'd bring it in person in case the wires for your high-speed Internet access got cut."

"Well, you didn't have to cross enemy lines," Ava told her. "Yet."

"Besides," Liza said, "I wanted to see you instead of just yakking on the phone."

"Yeah." Ava nodded. "Thanks."

Her phone started ringing again. "What do you bet this is another Killamook coward trying to pull an ad?"

Liza drove home, but she didn't get much accomplished once she got there.

In the course of a couple of days, she'd first put Bert Clements's badge on the line, and then stirred Ava Barnes into a course of action that could endanger her job.

With friends like me, Liza thought, ruefully shaking her head, *who needs enemies?*

She tried to come up with a few additional pieces for her column, only to butcher the puzzles through inattention.

The longer it took to get each sudoku to work, the shorter she got with Michael until he finally left to take a walk. Then she scolded Rusty until she finally decided to take *him* for a walk.

The afternoon was clear and cloudless, but Liza's skin crawled with that electric sensation that usually came between the thunderheads piling up and the first stroke of lightning lancing down.

Something had to be coming, she just wasn't sure what.

Leading Rusty past Mrs. Halvorsen's house, she noticed her neighbor's bus-sized Oldsmobile parked in the driveway. Then the door opened, and Mrs. H. waved her in.

"We came back for a quick bite to eat." The older woman's color was high, and she looked sprightlier than she had in a long while. "Then it's off again. Suppertime is a good chance to catch people at home and get their signatures."

She ushered Liza in. "We'll have something for you, too," she assured Rusty.

Buck and Alvin sat at the kitchen table, overstuffed sandwiches in front of them, their plates mounded with coleslaw and a big green pickle. Michael sat with the same setup, giving Liza a shamefaced wave.

"You were right to escape," she told him. "It was getting too close to tell who'd snap at you worse—whether Rusty or I would."

When she went to help Mrs. Halvorsen at the counter, she got chased to a seat. A moment later her neighbor deposited a supersized sandwich in front of her, then put down an equally large one for herself, which she tucked into with gusto.

"Mmmmph!" Mrs. H. chewed and swallowed. "I forgot."

She returned to the counter, rustled around in paper wrappings, and came up with several pieces of turkey, which she wrapped into a loose roll. "Here you go, Rusty."

Mrs. H. tossed the turkey, and the dog made it disappear in midair.

The human diners might not have been as quick to devour their meals as Rusty, but they were as thorough.

Liza sat back with a sigh of repletion as Mrs. H. filled her coffee cup.

"Just a half," Liza said. Experience had taught her that her neighbor favored a high-octane brew. She took a sip and puffed her cheeks in a silent whistle.

"After stoking the furnace, I want to make sure my thermostat is up," Mrs. Halvorsen confessed. "It wouldn't do to poop out—not when we're going to Killamook this evening."

Liza couldn't help her smile. "Now there's something I'd like to see." She could just imagine Mrs. H. turning up at people's doors with the large, implacable-looking Buck on one side and roly-poly Alvin on the other, probably looking as though his feet hurt.

"From the look of all those piles of paper in the living room, you've already collected a lot of signatures," Michael said.

"We need as many as we can get, and then some," Mrs. H. looked downright severe as she answered. "Those people are sure to challenge every name they can."

Her guests had to hide smiles to hear the Killamook machine referred to that way.

Looks as if "those people" will have to try pretty hard to get the better of Elise Halvorsen, Liza thought.

Buck suddenly spoke up. "Langley," he asked Michael, "would you mind staying here while we're out?"

He nodded toward Mrs. H.'s living room and the signed petitions stacked there. "I'd feel better having someone around to keep an eye on them."

"Uh—sure," Michael said, taken aback.

Liza just shook her head in admiration for Buck's clear-eyed, if cold, assessment. They were dealing with a bunch of crooked political types, after all. These guys were past masters of the art of the dirty trick.

"I'll stay with you," she offered, giving Michael a smile. "Double the guard."

Michael looked a little less spooked. "And we have Rusty to watch the perimeter."

That got a general laugh.

Mrs. H. graciously allowed her guests to take care of the dishes. Then she, Buck, and Alvin said good-bye and went off to do battle for truth, justice, and democracy.

"So," Michael said after the door swung shut, "what are we going to do now?"

"What have you got in mind?" Liza asked.

"Did you ever get to see the guest room upstairs?" Michael's eyebrows started waggling almost in semaphore.

"Yes, I've seen it," came her reply. "I even tested out the bed, so I don't need to try it again." She shot him a look. "Especially since I don't think Buck would appreciate us messing up his room."

"Did you say messing *in* his room?" Michael teased.

"Come watch TV," Liza told him. "We need to keep alert in case any of those political operatives come to mess with Mrs. H.'s petitions."

Michael sighed. "I think we can catch some sort of news show."

They barely got settled on the couch when Liza's cell phone began bleating. She checked the ID screen—Sheriff Clements.

Her hand wavered a little as she raised the phone to her ear. But her voice sounded steady as she said, "Sheriff, I hope this won't be unpleasant news." She glanced uneasily at the TV.

"Part of it is good news for you," Clements told her. "It looks as if you can be officially crossed off the suspects list."

"I . . . guess that's good," Liza replied. "But from the sound of it, there's more."

"You see, there was a small window of opportunity where we couldn't place Chad Redbourne, and you could conceivably have caught up with him," the sheriff explained. "But now we know where he was."

"And where was that?" Liza asked.

"At close of business today, a delegation of local bankers

came to talk to me," Clements said. "Seems they were getting questions from several different quarters about their financial dealings with the Party. That led to some questions among themselves—and finally sharing their information with me."

Liza tried to cut to the chase. "So what exactly was Chad doing?"

"Making withdrawals from various Party accounts," Clements replied. "Between two hundred to three hundred thousand per bank. All in all, he walked off with something in the neighborhood of a million and a half dollars."

14

"Well, in these days of trillion-dollar bailouts, that sounds like a drop in the bucket," Liza said into the phone.

"I suppose so," Clements agreed. "But it probably represents years of chiseling away at the twenty million bucks the county has to get by on each year."

"So now you have a whole new motive to work on for Chad's death." Liza made shushing motions as Michael looked up and was about to say something. "The question is how did he manage to make off with so much?"

"After all his years of service, he was something of a trusted employee in the machine," the sheriff replied. "It's a problem finding good help. Often it comes down to a choice of filling a job with someone loyal but incompetent, or competent but ambitious. After all, you don't want your underlings using their positions to create a power base to unseat you."

"And which was Chad?" Liza asked.

"He was that rarest of men," Clements said, "competent but controllable."

Liza thought back all those years—to all the times she saw Chad flinch whenever J.J. turned up. And when she'd seen him in his office just a few days ago, Chad admitted that he had no stomach for the rough-and-tumble of the courtroom. Oh, yeah, the Pauncecombes would have no problem controlling him.

"Since he was useful and dependable, he got tapped for a variety of jobs—including bagman," Clements went on. "He was cleared to use all sorts of accounts. The bankers weren't surprised to see him making withdrawals—it was just the size of them. But all Chad had to do was hint darkly that John Jacob had something big in mind, and they came up with the cash."

"Something like a quarter of a million apiece," Liza shook her head. "Looks like Chad decided to get ambitious somewhat late in life."

"Yeah," the sheriff said. "Right before it ended."

"At least you've got a whole new motive for the killing." Liza tried to joke. "If you see anybody buying themselves a fleet of Cadillacs—"

"I'm just grateful that it's distracted the boys in the machine so they haven't been concentrating on making life difficult for me." Clements gave a dry laugh. "Hell, they may even have to come to me and ask nicely if I'll look into it for them."

"Well, good luck with all of that," Liza said. "I don't know if she's been formally in touch with your people, but Mrs. Halvorsen has organized a petition drive for you. She got a little steamed when Chad's replacement invalidated all the previously collected signatures."

"My campaign manager called me about the saturation campaign. Frankly we were a little worried that it might be some kind of dirty trick by John Jacob and company. It's a relief to hear that it's for real."

They said good-bye, Liza clicked her phone shut, and then she turned to Michael, telling him about the missing million and change.

As she spoke, her mind was racing the way it usually did when she finished up a sudoku. Was this the missing piece of the puzzle that finally allowed the picture to make sense?

"So now we've got an explanation for the packed bag," Michael said when she'd finished her update. "Although it seems one piece of luggage is missing—the boodle bag."

Liza frowned, still unable to get everything to fit together. "We—well, I—had thought that this was a case of kill first and ask questions later. After killing Chad, the murderer would have found the packed bag as a nasty surprise—something to be gotten rid of quickly. That's why the stuff was so messily returned to the dresser."

Michael nodded. "But if we take the money as a motive, then the killer must have known that Chad was getting ready to leave town."

"Here's another question," Liza said. "Why go to all the trouble of faking a suicide?"

"To gain time?" Michael suggested. "It certainly confused the issue."

"But gain time for what?" Liza pressed the issue.

"The obvious answer would be for a getaway," Michael replied. "I guess the sheriff will be looking for anybody who took off on a sudden vacation."

Liza shifted on the couch in annoyance. "But was the suicide necessary? I mean, we only found out about the missing money now."

"The killer couldn't be so certain about the bank managers being reticent. And you yourself saw that the machine might have learned earlier—with J.J. Pauncecombe and Oscar Smutz visiting the bank."

Liza nodded, but reluctantly. Some parts of the machine might have known. But given John Jacob's way of dealing with the bearers of bad tidings, had the news made it all the way up the food chain?

"Still, she said, "it was a tremendous risk, hanging around the murder scene—not to mention actually having to move and pose the dead body." Remembering her first glance of Chad's hanging form, she shuddered.

But she didn't stop talking because something else was bothering her. "Whoever committed the murder had to have spent a good amount of time around Chad's place.

They had to know about the folly and about the steel piping around the inside. Otherwise why would you trundle the dead body and a rope all the way out there? There might be nothing to hang him from."

Liza stared at the TV screen, but didn't see anything. Or rather, what she was seeing was stuff that had happened almost twenty years ago, visions of the guys on the football team jostling Chad Redbourne.

"I keep going back to that Halloween prank in high school," she said at last. "Whoever rigged that tackling dummy had to know the same things as the killer who faked the suicide."

"It's not like cracking the genetic code," Michael objected. "Two separate people might have stumbled onto the same bits of information."

"Or maybe one person did it. Or one person heard about it from another," Liza conjectured.

Michael hunched his shoulders a little. "All right," he said in a resigned tone of voice. "Why don't you give Kevin a call? He was on the team, wasn't he?"

Liza dug out her cell phone again.

As luck would have it, Kevin didn't have any pressing business at the Killamook Inn right then. Hearing that there were new developments in the case, he readily agreed to come over and talk.

He arrived in about half an hour in his management casual outfit, a linen jacket over an open-necked shirt and a pair of pressed denims tailored to look like trousers instead of jeans. The pants alone probably outpriced everything that Michael had on.

Kevin looked around with an odd expression on his face as Liza held the door and he walked into Mrs. Halvorsen's living room.

"I'm trying to think of the last time I was in here," he said.

From the moment Kevin came in, Michael stood smiling at him—at least, his teeth were showing. When Rusty made a face like that, he usually added a growl. "Yeah, I guess that would be hard," Michael said, "since the last time you came in, you were dead drunk."

"So were you," Kevin shot back.

Liza rolled her eyes. Her two former beaus had barely been in the same room ten seconds before the testosterone wars began.

"I didn't get a chance to tell you why Mrs. Halvorsen is out," she began, trying to calm things down. "She's mobilized a whole bunch of friends to collect signatures on nominating petitions for Bert Clements—and for Ray Massini. I only mention it because apparently she didn't contact the sheriff's official campaign, and they thought this was something from the Pauncecombe arsenal of dirty tricks."

"I hadn't heard," Kevin said, "but I'm sure Ray will be glad to get the news."

Michael headed toward the kitchen, but paused in the doorway, looking back. "Hey, Kevin, you want a snack? I think Mrs. H. left some coffee, and maybe we could rustle up some cookies." He grinned. "Hanging out in somebody else's house—it's like being back in high school, isn't it?"

Kevin paused before answering, examining Michael's comment for possible barbs.

"I thought that was the best way to set things up," Michael went on, "because Liza wants to take you on a stroll down memory lane."

If looks could kill, the one Liza shot at Michael should have left him shriveled up on Mrs. H.'s carpet.

"I wanted to ask you more about Chad Redbourne," she said. "I just saw him for the first time in umpteen years a few days ago. You've been here in Killamook, and like it or not, you've seen some of the politics going on."

She took a deep breath. "Did you get any sense of what Chad was like? I mean, socially?"

Kevin shook his head. "His whole family was—well, weird. The mother was a prime social climber. My aunt and uncle lived about three blocks over, and everyone was excited when the Redbournes moved in. When they saw that fancy terrace going up, people figured that was going to be the party spot of the neighborhood.

"But no, the invitations all went out to ritzier parts of town. Problem is, none of the First Families of Killamook was interested. And when the Redbournes finally set their sights lower, none of their neighbors wanted anything to do with them, either."

"Whoa, I'd never heard that story," Liza said.

"You should ask Mrs. H. She and my grandmother used to talk about that all the time when I was a little kid."

"That whole fancy setup, going to waste," Liza mused.

"They tried it again when Chad got older," Kevin pointed out. "Figured if they got the kids over, they might make social points with the parents."

Liza made a face. "That worked out pretty well." She remembered her dad dropping her off at the Redbournes, insisting that it was impolite not to respond to a mailed invitation.

In spite of the magnificent setup—hell, the Redbournes had even sprung to have the first couple of parties catered— she had a hard time imagining more boring evenings. Turnout had been sparse, mainly class losers and kids with parents like Liza's who cared about etiquette. None of the cool kids or the social kids ever attended.

"How about later—when he grew up?" Liza asked "I figure you saw your share of political hoedowns. The inn must have hosted a fair share of them."

Kevin smiled wryly. "More than I'd like, to tell the truth." He thought for a moment, as if he were going over guest lists in his head. "Whenever the big boys held a fund-raiser, Chad was there. But otherwise, he was just a glorified worker bee. The cool kids still pretty much ignored him."

"Still sounds like high school," Michael interjected.

"Michael!" Liza shot him another look.

But Kevin only shrugged again. "Probably true, in a way."

Michael responded with an evil smile "Well, the school board is going to face a big budget cut."

Kevin's brows drew together. "What do you mean?"

Liza explained the news she'd gotten from Sheriff Clements—how Chad had drained money from the Party accounts.

"I guess that explains some of the grousing I've been hearing on the grapevine," Kevin said. "Not everyone working for the county is a loyal minion of John Jacob Pondscum. But if you want to keep your job, you go along, make contributions, and so forth."

"So?" Michael asked.

"So I've been hearing stuff for the last day or so about a special assessment—no explanation why, but everyone is expected to donate. All the big boys are saying is that it's necessary."

"I guess it is, if their coffers have taken a big hit," Liza said.

"Yeah, but when the news finally gets out to the rank and file . . ." Kevin paused. "The way politics is played around here, it runs on money and favors. And nobody's going to think it's a big favor to have the bite put on them over and above the usual take."

He smiled. "Maybe Mrs. H. and her friends are just the tip of the iceberg. At long last, people may be getting tired of the Killamook machine."

"Be nice to think so, wouldn't it?" Michael said doubtfully.

"So." Liza rode over his comment, trying to steer the conversation back to where she wanted it. "Chad didn't get to throw many parties, political or otherwise, at his house?"

"Many?" Kevin snorted. "I think the word would be 'any.'"

"That's what I thought." Liza's voice got a bit quieter now. "So how did the killer know about all the stuff at the Redbourne place?"

"Stuff?" Kevin said.

"The killer had to be familiar with the Redbourne place to know about that architectural folly," Michael interrupted impatiently. "And Liza thinks the killer would have to know the place intimately, figuring out how to rig that phony suicide."

"Intimately," Kevin repeated.

Michael snapped his fingers. "Keep up with us, Little Sir Echo."

Liza glared another unspoken "shut up" message.

"It wouldn't be easy to find the Grotto, for instance," she pointed out.

Kevin nodded. "Not with the trees and stuff. My uncle used to say that from spring to late autumn, he didn't have to look at his neighbors at all."

"So the killer had to know where it was—and know what was inside." Liza spelled it out. "Chad was strung up from some interior wiring conduit—just as the tackling dummy was set up years ago. So I'm asking—who knew that much about the Grotto?"

"That whole dummy thing—that was a hundred percent J.J. Pauncecombe," Kevin insisted. "He used to brag that he knew more about that damned beehive than the Redbournes did. He'd gone over every inch of the place—while going over every inch of most of the cheerleading squad."

He looked over at Liza. "You must have heard what J.J. said, that Chad had the best make-out spot in town—and nobody to take there."

Liza nodded. The first time she'd visited, Chad's mom had sent him off to take Liza on a guided tour of the Grotto. If his face had glowed any redder, she'd have been able to read in the dimness of the stone beehive. So it seemed that even Chad had heard.

"Well, J.J. wasn't about to let a place like that go to waste. He made it part of his private slang, 'Goin' in the *grot*-to,'" he mimicked. "He turned it into one of those whaddayacallems—double entries."

"That's bookkeeping," Michael told him. "You mean double entendres." He looked at Kevin carefully. "And there's something you're not telling."

Kevin looked uncomfortable. "He talked it up so much, other people used it."

"Did you?" Michael asked.

Liza glared at him yet again. But when she glanced over at Kevin, her jaw nearly dropped. Tall, lean Kevin, who always looked as if he could whip his weight in wildcats, had sort of hunched in on himself. "I always thought it was creepy."

"That's not exactly a yes-or-no answer," Michael said.

Kevin muttered something and then looked at Liza. "It was sort of a bet."

"What was?" she asked.

"I was talking with Brandy about finding my way through the woods—even then I was pretty good at it.

"She asked if I could do it at night without a flashlight. When I said yes, Brandy told me she'd left a ring in the bee-hive. If I could get it back that night, she'd give me a reward. There was a place where I could park my car behind some bushes on the opposite side of the block. If I went into the trees there, could I find my way to the Grotto?"

"Did you?"

"Yeah." Kevin kept his eyes trained on the floor. "And when I got there, Brandy was waiting for me. *She* was the reward. She had a lantern in there and an old blanket hung from that conduit to block any light from coming through the doorway."

"So what did you do?" Michael wanted to know.

Kevin went a bright red. "I ran. Left my car and just got out of there." He shook his head. "If the place was creepy before, it got a lot worse after that."

"When was this?" Liza demanded.

"Spring of junior year," Kevin replied.

She looked at him in silence for a moment. Up till then, Brandy had pretty much ignored her. After that, she'd gone out of her way to make life difficult for Liza. Hell, Brandy hadn't even gone out for class president until Liza started running.

Liza had a brief fantasy of strangling Kevin—and an

even stronger one of strangling Brandy. *Michael writes mysteries,* she thought. *I could ask him for a way to do it without being caught.*

On the other hand, asking an almost-ex-husband for a way to murder someone who almost seduced a past and sometimes present boyfriend probably worked better in soap operas than in real life.

Liza glanced at her watch. "Time for the evening news."

That ought to defuse some of the tension—and hopefully, distract Kevin and Michael from their continual sniping.

She bent over, manually switching on the TV. The screen immediately showed a station anchor with perfect teeth, blond hair moussed into short spikes . . . and a slightly rattled expression as he departed from the prepared script on the teleprompter.

"And now in a breaking story, we go to political reporter Evan Blair at the Killamook County Courthouse."

A balding guy with a bulldog chin and a microphone stood on the courthouse steps. "Todd, in a shocking development to the Redbourne murder case, Killamook DA Cy Langdon announced an indictment against local political godfather John Jacob Pauncecombe, the leader of Langdon's own party."

15

"What the . . ." Liza froze, still half-crouched in front of the TV set, staring at the screen as if the newscasters had suddenly switched to Lithuanian.

"Hey, Liza," Michael called from the couch. "Much as we enjoy the view, we'd like to look at the television, too."

Liza hurriedly straightened and stepped away.

"I don't get this at all." She turned to look at Michael and Kevin. "Sheriff Clements was just on the phone with me. Why would he tell me about Chad withdrawing all that money and not mention the fact that his people had arrested Pondscum Senior?"

"Maybe that's because he didn't arrest old John Jacob," Kevin said slowly. "Cy Langdon just said the old man had been indicted."

"So what's the difference?" Liza wanted to know, but she saw Michael nod in understanding.

"The cops investigate a crime, assess the suspects, develop a case, and then it's up to the district attorney to decide whether it's strong enough to go to trial. But sometimes—"

"Usually for political reasons," Kevin put in.

"The DA will bring a case to trial even if the police work is incomplete or shaky," Michael finished. "And yes, often it has to do with politics—the need to get re-elected, or because local feelings are running so high that the home folks have to see that something, *anything*, is being done."

Kevin picked up the conversation ball. "Cy has a couple of years to go on his term in office. And I haven't seen any torchlight processions demanding action in Chad's case. There is a certain amount of pressure to get this thing sewn up, though—and quickly, too. Every day Chad's case drags on, more light gets shone on the Killamook machine—and Cy and his pals look worse and worse. If Chad's death can be presented as a crime of passion, not something political, the DA probably hopes a lot of embarrassing stuff can be swept under the rug."

"And everybody remaining can close ranks and point a finger at the criminal." By now, Liza pretty well knew the emergency operating procedure of the Killamook machine by heart. "One question, though—why on God's green earth would John Jacob Pauncecombe go along with that?"

"That has everything to do with a different political pressure on Langdon," Kevin replied. "He's not just the DA. He leads a faction of Killamook politicians who aren't exactly on the same page with John Jacob when it comes to the next generation of leadership for the machine."

"You mean, he wants to take over after the old man retires rather than having this 'J.J. the younger' character take the reins," Michael said.

Kevin nodded. "So if this deal works, John Jacob is out of the way, and Cy is the guy who saved the machine. What's that line they used to say about politics? 'To the victor—'"

"'Goes the spoils,'" Liza finished. "The only thing is, this missing money may spoil Langdon's angry-lover scenario."

"Maybe that's one of the embarrassments the DA wants to sweep under the rug," Michael suggested.

"Still sounds kind of weird," Liza said, shaking her head.

"Or desperate," Kevin added with a frown.

They put aside further discussion at the sound of a car pulling into the driveway. Liza looked out the front window to see Mrs. H.'s Oldsmobile coming to a stop.

"Well, here come our professional consultants," she reported. "I guess we can ask them."

Alvin, Buck, and Mrs. Halvorsen entered and said hello to Kevin. "So, were you having a little party while we were out?" Mrs. H. asked with a laugh.

"Shades of high school," Michael muttered.

Liza explained why she'd invited Kevin over and brought the others up to date on the latest wrinkle in the case.

Michael looked at Buck and Alvin. "So what does it mean when the DA goes off on his own like this? Kevin suggested that it was politics—that this Langdon character was getting rid of the boss so he could step up."

"Politics is always possible, whenever the DA is elected." Buck frowned in thought. "Or he could just be playing hardball. I've seen prosecutors put together a funky case on one family member to squeeze something out of another."

"So what are you suggesting?" Liza asked. "Langdon is actually going after J.J.—but he's arresting the old man instead?"

"Maybe the DA wants to see what happens," Foreman suggested. "From what we've seen, the father has motive—Redbourne was having a fling with the wife. But from what you just told me, the son had the knowledge of the crime scene to try and fake a suicide."

Alvin spoke up. "Whoever the prosecutor is after, his case seems awfully weak. Any halfway competent defense attorney could kick it to pieces." A speculative gleam appeared in his eyes. "I wonder if these Pauncecombes are looking for representation . . ."

"Alvin," Michael warned, "I don't think Michelle

Markson would look kindly on the idea of you acting as mouthpiece for the enemy."

The so-called Lawyer to the Stars quailed at that possibility.

Mrs. Halvorsen looked up from the couch, where she'd sat down to organize a stack of signed petitions on the coffee table. "Those Pauncecombes may be big shots, but they're not good men."

She glanced over at Liza and Kevin. "Do either of you know how the first Mrs. Pauncecombe passed away?"

Liza dredged through her memories. "I was in seventh or eighth grade, I think. J.J.'s mom died in a car accident, didn't she?"

Mrs. H. nodded with a sour expression. "Yes, that's all that nice people would say."

"Are you suggesting that there was foul play involved?" Buck Foreman immediately had his cop face on, gearing up to investigate a twenty-something-year-old cover-up and murder.

"What?" Mrs. H. looked momentarily taken aback, then gave a sarcastic laugh. "No, I'm not suggesting that she was killed. I'm saying she was smashed."

She shook her head. "My Albert, God rest his soul, would do anything his company asked him to do—even if that meant taking me out for an evening of rubber chicken at some political do. And at every one of those I went to, Edith Pauncecombe wound up falling-down drunk."

She made a face. "Nobody noticed, of course, or so we pretended. It would be bad manners. But people talked about it—and other things.

"The father would chase anything in a skirt. I can remember him making the rounds in dining rooms, his tuxedo a little too tight, his face red, a scotch on the rocks in one hand and a cigarette in the other, just certain he was irresistible. The son turned out the same way."

Tell me about it, Liza thought, remembering what Kevin had just said about their high school days.

"Maybe that would have been different if Edith had anything to say about it, but of course, she wasn't there." Mrs. Halvorsen shook her head. "She may have driven into a tree, but that was because her husband drove her to drink with all his floozies."

"Do you think John Jacob cheats on Brandy?" The words just sort of popped out of Liza's mouth.

Mrs. H. raised her eyebrows in a "Who knows?" gesture. "That's what I hear. Although I also hear that she's not the type to sit pining—or drinking—at home. What's sauce for the goober—"

"I think that's 'goose,'" Alvin put in.

"I mean, you know that she and the son had a thing—of course you do, you were in school together," Mrs. H. said to Kevin and Liza. "Well, rumor has it that they still get together, although that sounds a bit tacky to me."

"So let me guess—did this Brandy wind up being voted Miss Popularity?" Buck asked.

"Actually, she wound up student vice president," Liza growled.

"Well, it seems as if there's a lot of stuff hiding in the bushes," Alvin said. "I guess we can expect this indictment to flush some of it out."

"From the stink it's going to raise, it might be better if it all went out the sewage pipes," Kevin muttered.

I guess he's thinking about his pal Ray and indiscretion on the other side, Liza thought.

"Well, at least we won't be hearing about any of this on the late-night shows tonight," she said. "They probably wrapped taping before Langdon made his announcement."

"Yeah," Michael said, "but there's always tomorrow."

The group broke up. Mrs. H. and her lodgers settled in for the evening, Kevin went home, and Liza and Michael walked next door.

As soon as she was safely in her kitchen, Liza went to the phone and punched in the number for the local sheriff's office. She knew that Bert Clements sometimes hid out in the Maiden's Bay substation when he wanted to avoid publicity.

All she got was a busy signal.

Sure, she thought grimly, *every media outlet for at least a hundred miles around probably wants a statement from him.*

For a long moment, she considered heading downtown and sneaking in through the back door at City Hall. No, that might just give Oscar Smutz another chance to beat his drums.

Then Liza realized she might have another backdoor access to how Sheriff Clements was taking the district attorney's ploy.

She punched in the number for Ted Everard's cell phone.

"Why, Liza, what a surprise," Ted said when he heard her voice. "Are you sure you're okay? Your dialing finger is all right? I expected you to call and try to pump me for info right after this Langdon character announced his end run."

Liza decided to ignore his sarcasm and get right into it. "Did you speak to the sheriff? What did he say?"

"As it happens, Sheriff Clements was busily trying to pick my brains—or rather, see if any of my CID experience could help him search for this money that Chad Redbourne made off with. I was making a few suggestions—not very confidently—about checking the grounds around Red-bourne's house when Brenna Ross came in and turned on the TV."

"How did Clements take it?"

"Let's just say if I had an egg I wanted to fry, I could have used his forehead. Of course, he hadn't rushed round to Langdon with this money thing. Said he wanted to nail it down before he talked to the county attorney."

"Translated, he knew Langdon was a fairly big wheel in the machine and didn't want the boys in Killamook to know that he knew about the money."

"Another case of the right hand not wanting the left hand to know what was going on," Ted agreed. "Langdon will want to quash any further investigation. If word of the money motive gets out, it will make his case look even weaker."

"Not to mention making him look pretty foolish," Liza said. "So is Clements still pushing on with the case?"

"He didn't exactly confide in me," Ted replied. "But I got the impression he had several deputies—people he thought he could trust—out pursuing leads."

"It's probably better if he doesn't find the money," Liza observed. "Once that news gets out, the politicians will all suspect one another of killing Chad and grabbing his loot."

Ted laughed. "If this indictment is anything to go on, they've started clawing at one another already." He paused. "So, do I get another invitation to lunch or something? I can stop by to talk to Clements and get all the latest dope."

Liza glanced through the kitchen door into the living room, where Michael sat making himself at home on the sofa, wielding the TV remote as if their almost-finalized divorce had never happened. She wasn't quite sure how she felt about that—or how she felt about going out with Ted right now.

"Um, got to check my schedule," she said.

As she said the word "schedule," her eyes fell on her computer in the corner, standing like a silent reproach to her failure to work consistently on her column. Her brain made another connection, though.

"Did you ever turn up Chad's collection of sudoku puzzles?" Liza asked.

That threw Ted off his stride. "His what?"

"Chad was quite the sudoku fan," Liza explained.

"Yeah, I got a certain inkling of that from his computers," Ted said.

"Chad created a whole bunch of puzzles—enough to publish as a good-sized book," Liza told Ted. "He had them collected as little booklets with the pages stapled together."

"As you know, I enjoy a good sudoku as much as the

next citizen of—what do you call it in your column?—Sudoku Nation," Ted said. "If they had been in his desk, I'm sure I'd have noticed."

"That's where he had them." Liza frowned, then her eyes opened wide. "But if he was leaving town, I bet he'd be taking them with him."

"Clements didn't mention them—I'm pretty sure he'd have kidded me about them—and about you." Ted tried to pass over his own loaded comment. "Maybe they disappeared with his million and change."

Liza had to laugh at that. "Yeah—his treasure." She couldn't help sounding a little wistful as she went on. "Still, would you mind asking about them—and if I could get some copies if they turn up? I'd like to put a couple in some columns—it's not often you get sudoku with a news hook, and it would make a nice remembrance for Chad."

Ted sighed. "Right. I'll inquire after getting a bunch of sudoku puzzles for you while subtly getting all the dope on how Sheriff Clements is proceeding with his secret investigation." He paused. "And if I succeed at that, I should get more than a lousy lunch. Now we're getting into the romantic dinner and drive bracket—and not at the Killamook Inn. I won't be able to enjoy my meal with Kevin Shepard glaring at me from the doorway."

"I'm not promising anything," Liza hedged. "I've got to get back to work."

"Yeah, yeah, always a good excuse," Ted groused. "I'll talk to you if I find out anything. Take it easy, Liza."

Ruthlessly shutting out Michael, the television, and her own thoughts, Liza managed to grind out a couple of decent sudoku. They weren't the most elegant puzzles she'd ever created, but they were certainly good enough for publication.

I wonder if Chad Redbourne's puzzles would be good enough to publish, she thought as she printed out final copies of her creations. After all, she'd gotten only a quick look at them there in his office. But the sheer bulk of the booklets suggested that some of Chad's output would be decent enough to see print.

Liza took the printouts over to Michael, intending to ask him to check them out. She blinked in surprise when she discovered the late news already on.

Michael recognized her expression and smiled. "Nothing much happened while you were visiting Sudoku Nation. Just a couple of foreign disasters, natural and political."

Even as he spoke, Cy Landgon's face appeared on the screen, announcing the indictment of John Jacob Pauncecombe. Then came the inevitable response, delivered by J.J. "We're shocked and disgusted by this obviously political prosecution—no, *persecution*—of my father, who has devoted his life to public service for Killamook County. Dad will meet with the DA tomorrow to show just how baseless these charges are."

The bald, bulldog-faced reporter they'd seen earlier in the evening appeared on the screen, looking a little nonplussed. "John Jacob Pauncecombe is presently in seclusion, but his wife asked to make a statement."

A teary-eyed Brandy Pauncecombe popped into focus. "The man I loved most in the world has been taken from me."

"That's laying it on pretty thick for a philandering husband," Michael quipped.

"And I do not intend to give any help to his murderer," Brandy went on, despite a quivering lip. "From now on, I'm going back to my maiden name of D'Alessandro."

Liza stared as the newscast went to commercial. "Did she just say what I think she said?"

"Spouses can't be forced to testify against one another," Michael said. "But it looks as if she's conducted the trial already."

"Trial, hell," Liza replied. "She's pushing for an execution."

16

As Liza predicted, the late-night shows had no jokes or comments about developments in the case—they'd filmed too early in the afternoon. All they had was one host apologizing that there was no exciting news from "Killacrook—excuse me, *Killamook* County."

The next morning's newscasts more than made up for that. First, the formerly monolithic façade of the Killamook machine fractured noisily into several factions. Pauncecombe loyalists angrily attacked Cy Langdon as an unprincipled political opportunist for his surprise indictment.

Langdon's supporters generally took a more statesmanlike view—"Let the DA do his job, and the facts fall where they may." But Liza caught a distinct whiff of hope that the Party's grand old man would get put away for the rest of his life while J.J.'s leadership aspirations crashed and burned along with his dad's reputation.

The local morning news shows featured fulminations from both sides, but a lot of the coverage went to Brandy Pauncecombe's—now D'Alessandro's—decision not to stand by her man. Or rather, that the man she decided to stand by was the deceased Chad Redbourne.

*Well, it was going to come out that she was sleeping
with him,* Liza thought. In fact, several Langdon surrogates
were almost gleefully harping on that fact as the motive for
Chad's death.

Pauncecombe's people looked pretty feeble on that
score, what with Brandy's public admission. Apparently,
however, they weren't ready to go after her as a scarlet
woman. The reason, Ava Barnes revealed over the phone,
had more to do with money than morality.

"This is something we couldn't put in this morning's
issue." Ava was almost chortling over the personal and
political bloodletting. "Most of the marital property wound
up in Brandy's name—some sort of financial or tax dodge.
The upshot, though, is that if John Jacob wants a good
lawyer to deal with this murder charge, he's got to play
nice—at least until he gets a chunk of his change back."

Liza had to hide a laugh of her own. Alvin was lucky
to have kept out of the Pauncecombe case—otherwise, he
might have ended up with a deadbeat client.

Brandy had a lawyer, too, a divorce attorney who went
on the air to present his client as suffering through a series
of husbandly infidelities before finding solace and love
with an old-school friend.

By afternoon, when Pauncecombe went to the Killamook courthouse (to "discuss matters," as his followers
put it, or to "turn himself in," as the Langdonites said), a
beet red John Jacob turned up with a public defender at
his side.

I guess the financial negotiations must be dragging,
Liza thought.

She noticed that J.J. ran interference with the reporters.
Given the expression of baffled rage on the older man's
face, Liza could understand the public relations aspects
of that decision. Just twenty-four hours ago, John Jacob
Pauncecombe had been top dog in this county. Now his
well-connected legal friends wouldn't touch him with a
ten-foot pole, and his wife was actively campaigning for a
guilty verdict.

Liza shook her head. *God only knows what might come out if he opens his mouth.*

Of course, the people having the most fun with the situation were the professional jesters of the Killamook Krew on the radio. Liza tuned them in after getting a call from Kevin. Jeff and Neal were in fine form, running various examples of political invective from both sides and making snarky comments.

In spite of the silliness, Liza found herself listening with interest. Was the owner of the station, Lawson Wilkes, working to discredit both factions while creating one of his own? Or was he angling for a better spot in the local hierarchy as some sort of power broker?

Liza tried to put all those thoughts out of her mind, turning to the computer to get some work done. She whomped up some columns to go with the puzzles she'd created, then took a break for lunch.

Looking out the kitchen window, she saw the sky clearing after an overcast morning. "I'm thinking of taking a walk with Rusty," she told Michael. "Want to come out for some fresh air?"

"Walking with that dog-dander factory of yours is not what I'd call enjoying fresh air," he told her. Jerking his chin at the computer, he asked, "Mind if I use your machine? I should check my e-mail and see what, if anything, is happening on the work front."

She half walked, half jogged with Rusty all the way to the beach. As usual, he interpreted any pickup in the usual pace as an invitation to race. The reel on the extension lead whirred madly as he'd dash out in front, then stop, looking over his shoulder in almost comical surprise that Liza wasn't keeping up with him.

They arrived at the bay front in an area empty of water- or sunbathers, so Liza freed Rusty from the lead to work off a little more energy loping around on the sand. He stopped every once in a while to sniff at something interesting but didn't manage to find any dead seagulls or other unpleasant things to roll around in.

Rusty contented himself with chasing after the tide with loud barks and then retreating as it came back in. After a while of this, he trotted back to Liza.

"Good boy," she said, petting him. "You certainly showed those waves who's boss."

Clipping the leash back onto Rusty's collar, Liza headed home.

She came into the kitchen to find Michael making iced coffee and listening to the radio. KMUC's political pundit was on, trying to keep the discussion to national issues while his callers vociferously went back and forth on the local split in the Party.

"Even with the stupid jokes, I liked the morning guys better than this stiff." Michael retrieved a container of milk from the refrigerator and then gestured to the sweating glass full of coffee and cubes. "Want one?"

In fact, he gave his to her and constructed a new drink for himself. Liza splurged on a little sugar to go with the milk, stirred up the mixture, and took a sip.

"By the way," Michael said as he poured more lukewarm coffee from the pot into his glass, "Ted Everard called. He sounded a bit surprised to have me answer."

Liza managed to avoid spraying coffee out her nose as she turned to face him. "Did he mention whether they found that sudoku collection of Chad Redbourne's?"

"He just asked that you call him back," Michael replied, "while sounding somewhat disappointed. I'm still trying to decide if that was because you weren't here or because I was."

Liza definitely was not going to get into that. She decided to try and keep things light. "Well, I'll ask when I call him back."

It took a couple of rings before Ted picked up on his cell.

"You're catching up with me just as we're in the middle of clearing out of Casa Redbourne," he said as loud voices gave orders in the background. "The good news is that we found your puzzles."

"With Chad's treasure?" Liza asked with a laugh.

"Not with his million dollars, unfortunately—that's the bad news," Ted told her. "The puzzles were in a manila envelope. We found it while shifting around the living room furniture. You remember how they had a made-to-order set of low bookshelves backing that big white couch?"

That cut Liza's laugh short. "Yeah, at parties they'd put bowls of chips and stuff on them—but nobody was allowed to eat them on the couch."

"Well, Chad must have put the envelope on the top," Ted said, "but it wound up slipping between the shelves and the sofa."

Liza frowned in thought. "I'd think a million bucks and change would take up a little more space than an envelope."

"If you piled up 150,000 hundred-dollar bills, you'd end up with a stack between five and six feet tall," Ted replied. "Taken with the other dimensions of U.S. currency, that would mass in at a volume around a thousand cubic inches—about the size of a large attaché case."

"Just like in the movies. And how much would that weigh in at?"

Ted muttered for a moment, doing some calculations. "Figure at one gram per bill, that would mean fifteen kilograms—more than thirty pounds."

"That's pretty big and heavy," Liza said. "What were you looking for, a false back on the bookshelves?"

"I thought maybe a slit in the back of the couch," Ted admitted, "with the cash substituted for the original stuffing."

"No luck, though?"

He sighed. "It wasn't in the freezer, or up the chimney, or in the toilet tank, either. We checked the basement, the attic, and the garage. There were no removable floorboards, and no loose bricks out in the terrace. And after a reasonably thorough going-over on the grounds, there were no signs of digging—except for what the squirrels had gotten up to."

"So what's next?" Liza asked.

Ted sighed. "Well, in light of the DA's—precipitate action, let's call it—Sheriff Clements had been holding off on any formal discussion of the missing money."

"In other words, he wanted to present the whole thing wrapped up in a ribbon in case Langdon shut him down," Liza translated.

"That's pretty much it," Ted agreed. "So what he's planning on now is doing up a written report and delivering it to the prosecutor's office. As soon as it's in Langdon's hands, he's going to run a press conference to make sure the information gets out."

Liza shook her head. Clements faced a "damned if you do, damned if you don't" choice. The Pauncecombes were already using the Party machinery against him. Annoying Cy Langdon by bringing up unwelcome evidence would turn the anti-Pauncecombe faction against the sheriff, too. But if he just turned the info over to Langdon and kept quiet, some rabble-rouser like Oscar Smutz could accuse Clements of not doing his job. Well, the last thing Liza would expect of Bert Clements was a cover-up.

"I guess the sheriff must really feel strongly about this," she said. "I know how he feels about talking with the media."

"That's why he's got that female deputy—Brenna Ross—doing the talking in Killamook while he lies low in the Maiden's Bay substation." Ted broke off. "Excuse me. Can you hold for a second?"

He must have put his hand over the cell phone's pickup. Liza could hear the bass rumble of a voice—the sheriff's, she guessed—but she couldn't make out any of the words.

Ted took his hand away. "The sheriff said he'd bring the booklets with him. You can copy a few of the puzzles in an hour or so."

"Tell the sheriff thank you," Liza said in surprise.

That cynical voice in the back of her head chimed in, sounding remarkably like Michelle Markson. *Why should he be so obliging when he's up to his ass in alligators?*

Such thoughts kept Liza a little distracted—not to mention somewhat nervous that Ted would start asking pointed questions about her choice in houseguests—until the end of the phone call. She hung up and looked around the kitchen, discovering that Michael had disappeared while she had been talking.

Liza drifted into the living room to find him slouched on the sofa, staring at the blank screen of the television.

"It's unhealthy, sitting in front of the TV with nothing on," she told him.

"Drafty, too, I guess," he replied. "Unless you decided to sit beside me with nothing on . . ."

"I think we'd shock the neighbors." Liza did sit beside him, fully clothed, and gave Michael a quick recap of what Ted had told her.

"So was he disappointed?" Michael asked.

"About not finding the money?"

"About not finding you home to answer his first call—or finding me instead," he said. "You said you were going to ask him."

"I forgot," Liza admitted.

The conversation pretty much died after that. They slouched side by side in silence until Liza stirred. "I'd better put on something a bit less disreputable."

"Getting dressed for Ted?" Michael just wouldn't let it go.

"I'd say it was more for Sheriff Clements," she replied. "A sign of respect for his office and all that."

She went upstairs and exchanged her sloppy top and shorts for a more decent T-shirt and a pair of khakis. *That way, I'll look as if I'm half in uniform,* she thought.

Coming back to the living room, she found Michael still on the couch.

"I'm going," she said.

"You'll be very early," he told her.

"Not if I walk."

Then you'll just be early, that snarky interior voice put in.

She gave Rusty a pat as he lay dozing in the pool of sunshine from the window and then started for the door.

"What about me?" Michael called after her.

So Liza came back and patted him, too.

The walk downtown was pretty uneventful. No media
trucks clogged Main Street in front of City Hall. Of course,
they were all in Killamook, getting the sheriff's news but
not the sheriff.

The deputy on duty passed her back to the inner
sanctum—or rather to the cramped room that served as
a combination interrogation chamber and branch office
for Bert Clements. He and Ted sat around the table that
the sheriff used as a desk when he wasn't looming behind
it to browbeat the truth out of alleged miscreants. Chad
Redbourne's puzzle collection was strewn across the table,
each improvised booklet enclosed in a clear plastic evidence pouch.

Clements greeted her with a nod. "Think you can tell us
a little more about these, Liza?" He tapped one of the booklets in its protective plastic. "Ten sheets, folded together
and stapled to make a book. Two puzzles per page, make it
forty per booklet, and I count two dozen booklets. With all
this, it's a wonder that Chad Redbourne found the time to
fix the county's elections, too."

"A labor of love," Liza told him. "At least, that's what
I figured when Chad pulled those things out of his desk
drawer. And by the way, it's not two puzzles per page. It's
one puzzle and its solution."

"Yeah," Ted said, "I noticed that."

"Did you try to work out any of them?" Liza asked.

"We thought we'd leave that to the professional," Clements said with heavy irony. "I'm afraid you'll only be able
to copy the puzzles that show."

"You're hoping to find incriminating fingerprints on
these?" Liza tried to hide her dismay. If that was the hope,
Clements was getting pretty desperate. "I mean, Chad
probably showed these to whoever came into his office."

"We're hoping he was a little more selective than that,"

Ted said. "Although our real hopes are on the envelope these booklets were found in."

"Was there a particular reason Redbourne showed the puzzles to you?" Clements asked.

"The obvious one—my column," Liza replied. "And then he asked me about the possibility of getting them published."

"I guess they will be, if you put them in the newspaper." The sheriff leaned his chair back on two legs. "And, of course, you'll let us know if you find anything surprising in them."

When Liza stared at him, Clements just shrugged. "After all, you've managed to wring some pretty surprising stuff out of puzzles like these before—phone numbers, account numbers . . ."

"Well, I don't think we're going to find how many steps from the old oak tree the treasure is buried," she warned. "Besides, Chad did all this long before he took any money from the banks. As I said before, these puzzles are just a labor of love."

"Oh, don't talk to me about love," Clements growled. "We had some people out canvassing with photo arrays on a more thorough basis than your single investigator could do—hitting all the shifts at the various motels, for instance. The results were waiting for me when I came in."

"And?" Liza asked.

"Oh, it's just dandy. The clerk identified Brandy Paunce—D'Al—whatever she's calling herself this week," The sheriff looked just about ready to spit. "The thing is, that clerk didn't pick out the picture of Chad Redbourne as the other person in the room."

He looked up at Liza. "For all her talk about finding true love, the lady was also bonking J.J. Pauncecombe."

17

"You don't look exactly surprised," Ted Everard said, looking up from his chair.

Liza shrugged her shoulders and threw out her arms. "My neighbor Mrs. Halvorsen mentioned hearing gossip along those lines. So surprised, no. But I am icked out a little. I mean, he is supposed to be her stepson."

"Technically speaking," Sheriff Clements rumbled. "But they had been going out together."

"Don't I know it," Liza mumbled. "In fact, the way I heard it, J.J. got Brandy the job that put her and the old man together." She made a face. "You don't think that even then, they—"

She vigorously waved her hand as if to fan away a bad smell. "Let's not even go there."

"It certainly took some nerve," Ted observed.

"Maybe not as much as you think," Liza said. "People are afraid of John Jacob Pauncecombe, but these days they seem more afraid of how he'll react if they tell him something he doesn't want to hear."

She shot a look toward the sheriff for confirmation, and saw him reluctantly nod. "As someone who got his head bitten off for unwelcome questions, I can attest to that."

"And it seemed to be pretty effectively managed, unless more canvassing turns up anything different," Liza said with a grin. "J.J. took Brandy north of town, Chad took her south."

"Sort of makes you wonder what you'd find if you took the picture collection due east," Ted suggested.

"Thanks, but we have enough complications as it is," Clements told him. "I just upset Cy Langdon's applecart by offering a money motive for Redbourne's death. Now I'm going to come up with an equally viable suspect."

He planted his elbows on the table, laced his fingers together, and rested his chin on his joined hands. "How do you think J.J. would react if he discovered that he wasn't just sharing Brandy with his dad, but with Chad Redbourne?"

"Messy," Liza said.

"Not just personally, but for the case," Ted added.

The sheriff slowly levered himself up from the table as if he were very, very tired. "Let's get what pages we can copied for you," he told Liza, and then paused. "And if by chance . . ."

"Right," she assured him. "If a clue leaps up and bites me on the butt, I'll be sure to call you."

Liza stretched the walk back home by stopping off at Castelli's for some more supplies. She arrived to find the status pretty much quo. Michael was still on the couch, and Rusty still snoozed on the carpet. She aroused interest in at least one of her housemates as she produced the photocopies of Chad's puzzles.

"I was thinking of just entering them and letting the computer do the solution," she told Michael, "but it might be more fun to solve them by hand."

So she just entered each of Chad's creations into the Solv-a-doku matrix and printed them out, sharing the stack with Michael.

For the next couple of hours, the house was quiet. It reminded Liza of Sunday afternoons early in their marriage. The entertainment budget was pretty small, but they could afford one of those digest-sized sudoku magazines.

They'd find the middle pages, bend the magazine back, and then tear it in half down the spine. Michael got one chunk, Liza the other, and they'd just lounge around and solve until it was time to make dinner.

Now, however, Liza kept glancing at her watch as she worked to finish off a fairly difficult puzzle.

The good news is that some of Chad's work is quite publishable, she thought. *The downside is that I'd like to finish this one before the evening newscasts start.*

She was in the backstretch by the time the news started, working through the chain reaction at the end of any sudoku. "If a two goes here, then a five goes there, and that leaves only an eight in this space," and so on. Liza had her solution by the first ad break and would have been quicker except she kept staring at the developing story. Brenna Ross, looking pretty good on camera, explained Chad's million-plus embezzlement in a brief clip. Then came Cy Langdon, fulminating about the Sheriff's Department releasing information that

	3					7		
					1	8		
7	9				5		6	
			7					5
4			9					3
2			6					
	2		8				1	4
		5	9					
		6				2		

might be important to a case (or rather, damaging to his). After that performance, though, an embarrassed Langdon had to try and explain how information about another possible suspect had leaked from his own office.

I guess John Jacob still has some followers working for the DA, Liza thought.

The operatic performance ended with Brandy D'Alessandro/Pauncecombe caught on the street by a camera crew, steadfastly reciting "No comment" in response to a series of awkward questions about her relationship with J.J. Pauncecombe.

"Tacky," Michael commented as the broadcast moved on to Congressional follies.

Liza had her reply interrupted by excited knocking at the kitchen door.

When she opened it, she found Mrs. Halvorsen flanked by Buck and Alvin. "Did you just see the news?" Mrs. H. demanded, her eyes just about popping from a mixture of outrage and titillation.

"Yes," Michael said, joining Liza at the door. "I was just saying how tacky I found the whole interview with Brandy."

"I don't know," Liza said. "Even not liking the woman, I ended up feeling sorry for her."

"I'd always heard things, but I find it sort of shocking to see it all over the TV," Mrs. H. complained. "Still, I guess you don't have smoke without fire."

Buck blinked, trying to follow that chain of logic. "Be that as it may, one thing is certain. The murder investigation is moving in very different directions now, and you certainly aren't considered a suspect anymore—which is why Michelle sent us up here in the first place."

"Yes," Alvin added with a portentous nod. "Our work here is done." Then he grinned at Liza. "Not that it hasn't been fun."

"Oh, you just liked being mistaken for Telly Savalas," Liza told him, "not to mention striking a blow for democracy in Killamook County."

"That was kind of different," Buck admitted. "But I think we should be getting back to L.A."

"Besides," Mrs. H. announced, "the petition drive is finished. We got more than twice as many signatures as required."

"Congratulations!" Liza hugged her neighbor.

"You didn't leave the petitions all alone next door, did you?" Michael asked.

Liza wasn't sure if he was joking or being serious.

Mrs. H. certainly took him seriously. "No, they were submitted to the elections office. Your friend Ava even sent a photographer."

That way Chad's successor whatsisname—Orem Whelan—can't claim deniability about the delivery of petitions or about the number of them, Liza thought. *Not if I know Ava.*

"Anyway," Buck said, "we've made reservations for the morning flight from Portland."

"I offered to drive them to the airport, but they won't hear of it," Mrs. Halvorsen complained.

Liza shared a quick glance with Buck, Alvin, and Michael. Getting to PDX and back would be a long drive for an older woman.

"I guess we'll just have to make some cab driver a very wealthy man," Alvin said.

"Don't be silly," Michael responded. "I'll give you a lift." He turned to Liza. "That is, if I can get a car."

"Oh, use mine." Mrs. H. grinned at her guests. "It's an old boat, but you'll certainly have more legroom than you'd get in Liza's compact."

With that settled, she invited Liza and Michael over for supper. "I've got a roast in the oven, surrounded by potatoes and onions," she said. "And with these two not around to eat up the leftovers, I'll be eating them for the next week."

"I've got some decent red wine," Liza said. Michael followed her back to the living room, where she rooted in some of the still-unpacked cardboard boxes in the corner.

"Nice wine rack," he kidded her.

"And a couple of nice bottles of wine," she replied, pulling them out.

The impromptu farewell celebration left everyone pleasantly full and slightly buzzed as they said good night.

Liza and Michael strolled across the lawn in the growing darkness. Rusty met them eagerly at the door—too eagerly.

"Guess who has to go for a walk," Liza said. "I know you have to get up pretty early for your date tomorrow morning. Do you want to turn in?"

"Not before I finish this," Michael replied, picking up the sudoku he'd been working on when the news started.

Liza took Rusty on a quick tour of the high-interest sniffing spots around the neighborhood, let him do his business, and returned.

Michael had returned to his spot on the couch. But a quick glance told Liza that he was working on a new puzzle.

"Did you get stuck, get bored, or get finished?" she asked.

	5		9					3
2		7					9	
			1	2				
			9				5	6
		6	5	7	1	9		
9	2		6					
			8	4				
	3					4		8
4					7	2		

He gave her a shamefaced smile. "Finished. But I thought I'd like to try another."

"So will I." Liza picked another puzzle from the pile, and they sat together in companionable silence again.

Michael finished his sudoku and then reached for yet another.

They finished at almost the same time, their hands brushing as they both went to the pile.

Both of them smiled. "We ought to hang these up side by side," Liza joked. Maybe it was seeing the puzzles beside one another, or maybe it was the agreeably muzzy feeling from all that wine with dinner.

Liza frowned and a question showed on her face. "How are these puzzles similar?"

Michael shrugged. "I don't know. What? They both have eighty-one spaces?"

Now he frowned a little, peering harder at the sheets of paper Liza held up. "It's not the number of clues, or the shape of the original puzzle."

Michael shook his head. "Okay, I give up. What is it?"

Liza grabbed his pen and began blacking out all the spaces on the puzzle but one. Then she did the same with the second puzzle and showed them to Michael again.

"Both of them have a one in the first space."

"Huh." Michael gave her a quizzical look. "I don't know that I'd really have noticed that."

But Liza was already going over the rest of the puzzles they'd done. "Here's another one."

Then she began stacking some of them. "Look in the last line of this one—and this."

"Now the one is in the final space of the puzzle," Michael said.

After a little more shuffling, Liza held up three more. "And here?"

"The one has moved to the lower-left corner."

Now Michael began sorting through the dwindling pile. "I've got a one in the upper right . . ." He laughed, holding up another sheet. "Here's a double-header—a one in the upper right *and* the lower left."

Liza regarded the little piles they'd created. "All the puzzles we did, and the number one appears only in a corner. What are the chances of that?"

"Ummmmm . . . one in nine?" Michael suggested. "That's the chance for any single space in a sudoku, after all."

"Okay," Liza admitted. "But in all of these? If there's a one in nine chance of getting a one in a given space, that means a nine-to-one chance of it *not* being a one."

Michael shrugged. "Well, you said that there were two dozen booklets with twenty pages each. That's two hundred and forty puzzles in all. With the booklets sealed in evidence bags, the sheriff could only photocopy the front and back pages. That's two for each of the twenty-four booklets—forty-eight in all."

Now it was his turn to frown.

"By the odds we just discussed, that seems kind of high. I'd have thought maybe there'd be twenty-four."

Liza nodded. Then she started heading for the kitchen.

"What are you doing?" Michael called after her.

"I'm calling Sheriff Clements and asking him to check the other puzzles when they open those bags." She stopped in the doorway and looked back. "He made me promise to get in touch with him if I found a clue in those puzzles."

"And this may be a clue," Michael said.

Liza nodded. "To what, I'm not sure. But it may be a clue."

She called the substation in Maiden's Bay. The sheriff wasn't there, but the deputy on duty had his orders and relayed Liza's call to Clements's home number.

When he answered the phone, Sheriff Clements sounded even more tired than he'd seemed just this past afternoon. But he rallied when Liza made her report. "I don't know what it means, either, but it does seem kind of strange," he agreed. Clements also promised to get a full set of copies to Liza when the booklets came out of their bags.

Her civic duty done, Liza came back to the living room to find that Michael had switched on the television with the volume down low.

"I thought you were turning in early," she said.

Slouched on the couch, he just shook his head. "All of a sudden, I don't feel like it."

They watched some cop show, but Liza kept losing track of the plot. Occasional lines of dialog stuck in her mind, but the scenes seemed to follow one another in an almost surreal pattern. She wasn't sure whether this was a result of too much wine at dinner, or whether her brain was attempting to assimilate all the bizarre information that had fallen into her lap in the past few days and make it into a tidy coherent picture.

I might be able to do that with sudoku, she thought, and not for the first time, *but real life is definitely not sudoku.*

They watched the late news come on, presenting basically a rehash of all the developments they'd watched earlier that evening. None of it presented Liza with the magical touchstone that forced everything to make sense.

Then the late-night show came on. Predictably, the host had a field day with all the new twists in the saga.

"Things are getting even more exciting in Killacrook County," he told the audience. "Now you know this all started out with a crooked politician being killed out there."

He paused for a second. "It might be a bigger mystery trying to find a politician who's *not* crooked."

The audience hooted approval.

"So yesterday, they indicted the political boss up there, the head crook, because it turns out that the dead guy was—how can I put this delicately? He was doing the horizontal two-step with the head crook's wife."

A general "Whoooooo!" came from the spectators. The host waved them down.

"It gets even better today. Turns out that the dear departed stole something like a million and a half dollars before he was killed. He might have gotten dead before he even had a chance to mention the money. Or the killer may have made off with the boodle, although that's hard to believe. A politician may kill, but steal?"

He raised his eyes with a pious expression while the folks in the studio howled.

"As for the boss, his wife says the dead guy was the love of her life, and she's not ponying up any money for hubby to get off the hot seat. Speaking of hot, here's a shot of the wife in her brief Hollywood career."

Somewhere, they had managed to locate a clip of Brandy in a tight, low-cut evening dress just as she was slipping the straps off her shoulders. A big CENSORED sign appeared across her chest.

"Seems like she's one of those trophy wives," the host went on, a bemused sort of smile on his face. "Although in this case, it seems like a trophy that goes from team to team. Besides hubby and the dead guy, she was also stepping out with her stepson."

Liza was glad the volume was down as scandalized laughter came from the TV.

The host stood shaking his head as the noise subsided. "Lost money, corruption, sex scandals—these guys should never have gotten involved in county politics. They're obviously ready for national office."

He smiled again at the audience. "I swear, folks, nobody could make this up." The comedian suddenly pulled a face as he looked directly into the camera. "At least not my writing staff."

Liza got to her feet to head for the kitchen again. This time she called Michelle Markson's cell number.

"Liza, dear." Judging from the tone of Michelle's voice, the wine had been flowing freely this evening for her, too.

"Have you been playing up this late-night war with the politicians up here?" Liza asked bluntly.

Michelle laughed. "No need, dear. I pointed them in the right direction and set the machinery in motion. I don't even need to tweak it anymore. It runs by itself."

18

Liza had the dream that night. It was a recurring almost-nightmare she'd had ever since she was a kid. It would start in a familiar setting, in this case a classroom at Killamook High. Everything was pretty much as Liza remembered, except for the gleaming control panel set into the top of the teacher's desk.

Fascinated, Liza inevitably touched something. That's when she discovered she wasn't in a room, but the cockpit of some enormous machine that rose up on towering legs and set off across the countryside, flattening everything that got in its way with gigantic feet. The metal behemoth's first step took out most of the high school's student body, which fled screaming across the parking lot.

As Liza frantically tried to find the stop button, the runaway monster crashed and crushed its way along Broad Street, leaving destruction in its wake. Then it smashed its way to the edge of town. Liza looked up from the fiendishly complicated control panel to see the Redbournes' folly—and their house—ground to wreckage under the huge robotic feet.

The uncontrolled behemoth bounded forward in block-sized strides along the highway. Liza thought maybe she could get it to turn into the lake, but it plowed along. Soon Maiden's Bay came into view. More wholesale demolition took place as the rudderless robot monster somehow made a beeline for Hackleberry Avenue and Liza's house.

The kitchen door opened, and out came Mom and Dad. Instead of running for their lives like sensible people, they attempted to shoo the monster away from their property. Liza was treated to a close-up vision of her terrified parents clinging together, even though they looked tiny as the huge metal foot descended upon them—

Liza sat up in bed, shuddering. She hated that dream, blaming it on the Japanese cartoons her mother had bought her as a kid, hoping to interest Liza in her mom's native language.

Gingerly, Liza rubbed her temples, where a headache already seemed to be throbbing. She spent extra time under the shower, but emerged still feeling unrefreshed.

The weather outside was foggy and misty, so Liza wore jeans and a sweatshirt as she padded barefoot downstairs. Michael was already gone, ferrying Alvin and Buck to Portland. In spite of her quiet tread, Rusty rose up from where he'd ensconced himself in Michael's bedding, always alert for the possibility of treats.

Liza gave him one, poured herself a cup of coffee from the pot Michael had left for her, and turned on the radio. KMUC's Killamook Krew might be sophomoric at best, but they also provided a window into the dark corners of the minds running the local political machine. And judging from last night's monologue performance, the boys on the radio had plenty of grist for their mill.

Listening to the would-be comedians, Liza decided that the Killamook machine's mental state was apparently schizophrenic. Noisy Neal was bouncing all over the place like a hyperactive second-grader, making mouth noises over the film clip of Brandy.

In contrast, Jeff sounded as if he were reading copy that had been vetted by the legal department.

The dysfunctional duo wallowed on until Neal used the phrase "Killacrook County" in one of his rants. The next commercial break ran three times longer than usual. As Liza listened to commercial after prerecorded commercial, she wondered what was going on behind the scenes at the radio station.

She got her answer when only Jeff came back on the air, sounding more shell-shocked than smart-assed.

"We—that is, I—would like to apologize to the good folks of Killamook for, um, taking the county's name in vain during this tragic period. I guess murder is no joke, and certainly the investigation has been stressful for a lot of people."

Certainly, Jeff's nasal voice sounded pretty stressed. "So Neal will be taking, um, a bit of a time-out at the station management's request, and we'll be continuing with the adventures of the Killamook Krew, just a little, er—short-handed."

The morning show limped along without its usual banter, with the best exchange coming between Jeff and the newscaster. "You can't get yourself suspended, Jeff," the news guy had pleaded. "I can only fill five minutes out of every hour. What will we do for the other fifty-five?"

Liza made herself some toast to go with her coffee and turned off the radio. She was just washing the breakfast dishes when the kitchen phone jangled. Grabbing a dish towel, she walked across the room and picked up the handset.

"We opened the evidence bags and looked at the puzzle booklets," Sheriff Clements announced. "All of them have ones in a corner."

"So it's not just dumb luck." Liza wasn't sure whether or not she should be pleased that her hunch had panned out.

"I guess Redbourne had a reason to do it." Clements's voice took on more of a sour tone as he continued. "Too bad we have no idea what that reason might have been."

"Maybe you should check in with a real crime-buster like Oscar Smutz," Liza suggested.

That got a snort of laughter from the sheriff. "Anyway, I had all the puzzles copied for you. They're in my office in Killamook." He paused for a second, then explained, "I have some people I need to meet here today. Suppose I leave an envelope for you with the desk deputy?"

"That would be fine," Liza said. "I'll get over there later today."

She hung up and looked down at Rusty, who simply sat watching her with his tongue lolling out of his mouth.

"No need to let the sheriff in on all the glamorous details of my exciting life," Liza told the dog. "I have to take you for a walk, and then do some laundry—wash your dander off poor Michael's bedding, or he'll sneeze his fool head off."

She went upstairs to put on her shoes, got a load of washing into the machine, and then got Rusty's leash.

The fog had cleared a bit, but the air was still misty as they stepped outside. Liza saw her next-door neighbor was also up and doing. Mrs. Halvorsen stood in her garden, a hooded Windbreaker keeping away the worst of the damp.

As soon as Rusty spotted her, he went bounding over with a low "Woof!" of hello.

Mrs. H. bent to pat his head.

"Digging for earthworms?" Liza asked with a smile.

"No, just looking and planning," the older woman replied. "That nice Mr. Foreman was kind enough to bring in the start of a rock garden."

Liza looked at the substantial pile of stones that had appeared in one corner of the garden plot. "I guess it was nice to have a strapping type to do some of the heavy lifting."

"I'll miss him," Mrs. Halvorsen said suddenly. "And that sweet Alvin."

Liza wasn't sure which surprised her more—Mrs. H.'s admission or the description of Alvin Hunzinger, cutthroat defense attorney, as "sweet."

Well, she certainly had a couple of very full days with Alvin and Buck, what with the investigation and then the petition drive, not to mention the rock garden, Liza thought. *I guess this would come as a bit of a letdown.*

Touched by the suspicion that her older friend might be feeling a little lonely, Liza said, "If you don't have anything more pressing than garden planning, how about a girls' lunch? I have to go over to Killamook to get something from the sheriff, and I wouldn't mind the company."

Mrs. H. beamed. "What a wonderful idea! I'll go in and get spruced up a little . . ." She broke off, looking at Liza's casual outfit.

Liza smiled at her. "I'll do the same, after I finish taking my friend here for his walk."

They made a quick round through the neighborhood, and when they got back, Liza climbed the stairs to find some more formal casual attire.

"Guess it'll have to be my car," she said when she got next door.

Mrs. H nodded. "Yes, Michael is making sure the Olds-mobile gets a little exercise."

They drove over to Killamook and down Broad Street.

"The sheriff's office is behind the courthouse," Liza said, not sure whether her neighbor knew where that office might be.

As they came close to the courthouse, they discovered vans decorated with TV station logos blocking the road.

"I guess the district attorney must have called another press conference," Liza said. Instead, they found the camera crews crowded outside the Sheriff's Department.

Liza's heart sank when she recognized several of the television reporters—they'd covered cases in Maiden's Bay where she had gotten involved.

"If I walk in front of those cameras, I'm going to become the story," she whispered to Mrs. H. "Would you mind going in to the front desk and picking up the envelope for me?"

Mrs. Halvorsen managed to get in and out just in time. No sooner did she rejoin Liza, the manila envelope clutched under her arm, than the glass doors swung open, and the Pauncecombes, father and son, walked out. A young guy with a cheap briefcase and an even cheaper suit that just about screamed "public defender" accompanied them.

The cameramen leaped into action, aiming their equipment at the young lawyer. "Ladies, gentlemen, I'm Randy Beale, representing Mr. John Jacob Pauncecombe and his son, John Jacob Junior. I'd like to make a brief statement. Both of my clients have faced accusations and innuendo regarding the death of Chad Redbourne. Today we offered the Sheriff's Department irrefutable proof that neither of these gentlemen was even in Killamook at the estimated time of death. We hope this will end—"

"Could you tell us where they were?" a skinny blond woman with a microphone shouted. On screen she looked ten pounds heavier, but in real life, she came across as almost skeletal.

Randy Beale blinked, losing his train of thought. "Excuse me, but this is not a press conference. I'm only giving a statement—"

Now the bulldog-faced newsman called out, "Could you amplify that statement? Specifically, with regard to where this alibi actually put your clients?"

"N-No questions," Randy stuttered even as he tried to enforce his ground rules.

"If you can't tell us where they were, it's not much of a statement," a third newscaster challenged.

"The sheriff was willing to accept it," Randy said.

"As long as he had enough facts to check it out," Bulldog argued. "We'd like the same opportunity."

"Where did they go?" another of the news reporters asked.

Others took up the cry. "Where? Where?"

John Jacob Pauncecombe took a step at them, his fists clenched. But the attack he launched was verbal. "You bunch of prying bleeps want to know where we were?" He hooked a thumb at J.J. "Genius here was shacked up with some bimbo at a motel in Glenwood."

A town to the east of Killamook, Liza thought. *We should have looked in that direction after all.*

"Why he didn't continue all the way to Portland and find a decent place for his bleeping, I don't know."

Pauncecombe glared at the cameras. "As for me, I was in bleeping Portland, at the bleeping ResusaGen clinic, getting treatment for E bleeping D. Because when you've got ED, you can't bleeping bleep! You can check at the motel and at the clinic—that should be enough bleeping information for all you nosy bleeps!"

The old man hurled F-bombs, S-bombs, and others with both hands, ignoring the winces and stares of the newspeople.

At the rear of the crowd, Liza grinned. She was pretty sure that even the best editing crew wouldn't be able to cobble that outburst into a coherent—or broadcast-worthy—sound bite.

At least he's up-front about it, she thought. What was it about political life? John Jacob, J.J., and even Chad were doing to whoever what the Killamook machine had been doing to the county for years.

Her grin faded as another thought sank in. If these alibis actually stood up, then the two strongest suspects in Chad's death would be off the hook.

Maybe some of the same thoughts must have passed through Mrs. H.'s mind as well. She laid a hand on Liza's elbow. "What will you do next?"

Liza shrugged. "Right now? I think we're supposed to have some lunch."

They escaped before the newspeople finished doing their taped wrap-ups and returned to Broad Street.

"Where shall we eat?" Liza frowned, looking up and down the unnatural perfection of the building façades. Across the street, a brave restaurant owner had tried for more of a café than an Early American ambience, opening his awning to shade a couple of tables on the street.

Liza and Mrs. Halvorsen crossed over and grabbed a table. Soon they sat discussing the merits of a sweet lettuce salad versus the cheese platter.

"Oh!" A deeper shadow fell over Liza's menu, and she

looked up to find Brandy D'Alessandro/Pauncecombe staring down at her. Brandy wore tight jeans and a tighter T-shirt, the winking scales on her gold snake belt creating a little light show as the sunlight hit them.

"Did you hear the news?" Brandy asked. "My skunk of a husband and his son told some BS story to the sheriff, and they're out."

"It would take more than BS to convince Sheriff Clements," Liza told her, but Brandy shook her head.

"They're in it up to their necks," she said. "Maybe they didn't do it themselves, but they could have it done."

"The way I hear"—or rather, the way she'd heard it from Ted Everard—"the Killamook machine has depended more on controlling people through money and favors than strong-arm stuff. Where would they find someone they could depend on to kill Chad?"

"How about that big creep Oscar Smutz?" Brandy demanded. "He's made a whole career out of cleaning up after J.J.—since high school. J.J. got in a fight with a college kid who threatened to have him up on assault charges. The deputy who answered the call was Smutz. He figured Big John Jacob would appreciate a little police initiative. So Smutz scared the other kid by saying he could just as easily have him up for assault with a deadly weapon—apparently, the college kid had picked up a pool cue. And that's how Smutz got into politics."

"Bending the rules, even leaning on someone, is a far cry from bumping someone off." Liza had a hard time imagining Oscar Smutz as a killer for hire. More to the point, how desperate would someone have to be to put themselves in the hands of an opportunist like Smutz to the tune of conspiracy to murder?

"They did it, and they're going to get away with it." Brandy grew almost tearful in her insistence. "And now they're starting on me. My lawyer called and told me to get out of the house. He might as well have told me to get out of town. I can't find a place to stay—people are too afraid of John Jacob now that he's out again. I saw him on

TV—he was so angry, they were bleeping out everything he said."

"So where are you going to stay, dear?" Mrs. H. asked.

Brandy gave a deep sigh, starting off all sorts of jiggles. "I dunno. If I can find someplace quiet—and safe—maybe I could sleep in my car."

"Nonsense," Liza's neighbor said staunchly. "I've got a spare bedroom. You can stay with me."

"You—what?" Liza had a bit of déjà vu to this morning's dream—the runaway machine whirling faster and faster along. She just didn't seem able to keep up with the latest developments.

"Sit down and have something to eat," Mrs. H. insisted.

"I don't have much in the way of cash," Brandy said hesitantly.

"I'll pay your freight," the older woman told her.

Liza must have had something for lunch, but she really couldn't have identified it with any certainty. Her food tasted like ashes in her mouth as she watched Brandy become Mrs. Halvorsen's new best friend.

Brandy's mention of financial troubles led to a discussion of money in general—and to Chad's million and change in particular.

"John Jacob was going crazy over that," Brandy reported. "Money is really the only thing he cares about."

"What about you and Chad?" Liza delicately asked.

Brandy shrugged. "Oh, he'd have been PO'd about that. But Chad of all people stealing from those accounts—that really hit John Jacob where he lived."

She started to sniffle again. "And maybe that will be the only punishment they'll face for killing Chad—having that money just disappear."

Leaning across the table, Brandy suddenly grabbed Liza's hand. "You're smart—I've heard how you solved murders and things. Why don't you really make them pay—find that money and make sure they don't get any of it back!"

Liza disengaged her hand, a little embarrassed by

Brandy's faith . . . and fervor. "I don't know if that's even possible. The sheriff has no idea where the money went."

The others finished their meals, but Liza left half her food on her plate.

"Is your car nearby?" Mrs. H. asked Brandy.

"Just down the block." Brandy pointed to a silver BMW.

Liza tried not to roll her eyes. Oh, poor Brandy, forced to rough it in a Beemer.

She drove home with the silver car in her rearview mirror. "Are you sure this is a good idea?" she asked Mrs. Halvorsen.

"I'm not going to let those two awful men bully that girl," Mrs. H. replied stoutly. "Besides, she told me she'd just lie low for a few days while she decides what to do next."

Liza left her neighbor with a silver Beemer in her driveway and a new houseguest bringing a single suitcase into the house. She noticed that the Oldsmobile was already parked, so it came as no surprise to find Michael on the couch. She thought he might be snoozing after rising so early, but instead he seemed to be sitting and waiting for her.

"I debated trying to catch you on your cell," he said. "Sheriff Clements had kind of a busy time—"

"Did you catch any of it?" Liza asked.

He nodded. "Lots of coverage on KMUC. Unless they were kidding around with the bleeping, your pal John Jacob must have one hell of a vocabulary."

She shrugged. "Sounded kind of repetitive to me."

Michael leaned forward on the couch. "Anyway, all the publicity that case has gotten caused a clerk from the Killamook post office to come forward. Seems Chad Redbourne was there late on the afternoon of the day he died, sending off packages."

"Packages?" Liza echoed.

"According to Clements, the postal clerk said they looked like little bricks, heavily wrapped."

"Oh, dear Lord," Liza muttered. "He was mailing off

stacks of money? Isn't that illegal? Or at least there's some sort of limit . . ."

"Yeah." Michael put on his tough gangster voice. "He'd be facing major time in the big house . . ." He reverted to his normal tones. "Oh, wait, he's dead."

"So can the postal authorities trace it?" Liza asked.

"In a word, no," Michael replied. "He didn't ask for tracking—or insurance for that matter."

Liza could just see that one. "The value of the package? Oh, about fifty thousand dollars."

"Chad just sent them parcel post, and the clerk didn't pay any attention to the addresses."

"Great," Liza muttered. "You think it will end up in the dead-letter office?"

"I think we'd have a worse wait than that," Michael told her. "The cash is in the mail."

19

"Let's try to be serious about this." Liza pulled the sheaf of papers from the envelope she'd carried into the house. "We know that Chad was doing something with a collection of nine-digit numbers—"

"Each of them beginning with the number one," Michael added.

"If we go with what the sheriff just told us, there may be a postal connection." Liza's voice faded off as she sank into thought.

"Zip plus four?" Michael suggested. "The original zip codes are five digits. Add four, and that makes nine."

Liza was already headed for the computer. "Let's see if we can get a national listing of codes."

She found a USPS website that let her input zip codes and get the town names associated with them. But after several minutes of Michael reading off the first five digits from suspicious rows and columns, she stopped typing.

"A bunch of these aren't even in the postal database," Liza said. "And the ones that are cover a swath of territory through Pennsylvania and upper New York State. It's like Allentown to Albany, with a whole lot of small towns in between. If he mailed off cash to all these places, was he planning a getaway or a road trip?"

Michael began whistling Johnny Cash's "I've Been Everywhere, Man" through his teeth.

Liza shook her head. "It was a nice idea, but I don't think it works." She got up from her chair and began pacing the living room floor—not easy when she had to evade both her husband and her dog. Finally, with a sigh, she headed for the kitchen.

"If you're going for a snack . . ." Michael began.

"I'm going for the car keys," she called back. "Maybe if I clear my head . . ."

She didn't finish the thought, swearing at the keys as they jingled out of her hand to the floor. Liza picked them up and headed back to the living room, where she took the sudoku copies from Michael's hands and stuffed them back in their envelope.

He now lay on the couch. "Want some company?" Michael's voice sounded drowsy, as if their abortive zip code search had drained his energy.

Well, he was up pretty early this morning to act as chauffeur, Liza thought. "Why don't you just take it easy?" she said aloud. "I don't think I'm fit to be with right now."

She debated telling him about Brandy Pauncecombe interrupting her lunch and moving in next door but decided her feelings were too complicated to discuss.

She went outside, climbed in behind the wheel, and used her key to start the car. Pulling out of the driveway, she clicked on the car radio. KMUC's afternoon pundit was on the air, pontificating on the meaning of the Pauncecombes getting back into society again. Apparently, the Party line was that everything would be normal now.

Liza drove aimlessly around for a bit, then found herself merging onto the highway. She exited at Killamook but avoided the downtown, making her aimless way through residential areas until she cruised past the Redbourne place.

She slowed for a moment, then drove past the driveway. But she made a right at the next corner and another right after that. The properties were just as big on the next block, with overgrown areas between the houses. How had Kevin quoted his uncle? From early spring till late autumn, they didn't have to look at their neighbors at all?

Liza found a space between a pair of bushes and pulled in. She was hidden not only from the neighbors but from any passing cars. She got out of the car. A sketchy sort of pathway led deeper into the trees.

It took a little walking and a couple of false starts, but she came out of the brush on the far side of the Redbournes' folly.

I wonder how I'd have felt sneaking over here back when I was in high school, Liza wondered, then shook her head and smiled. *Guess it would depend on what guy I was sneaking over with.*

Her mood changed when she came around to the front of the beehive. Apparently, the crime-scene tape was down from the entrance to the folly—or had the sheriff's people even bothered putting any up?

Chad's hanging form was gone, too, but Liza shuddered anyway.

Kevin is right about one thing, she decided. *This place is creepy.*

She hung back from the opening. Then, taking a deep breath, she stepped in. It was cooler inside the folly, even cooler than it had been under the canopy of foliage. Darker, too. She wrinkled her nose. Not to mention a bit musty.

Liza tried to take herself back to high school, to look through her younger self's eyes. The Grotto would have been newer then, but of course, it had been built to look ancient.

Not the most romantic spot, she thought. *But then, just about anyplace is Inspiration Point for a teenaged boy.*

She moved over to the long bench set against the far wall, the wooden piece's self-conscious rusticity softened by a set of floral-patterned cushions. They were on the thin side, made of plastic, the sort of thing Liza associated with backyard furniture.

Not faded, she thought. Closing her eyes, she tried to
bring up the image of her brief tour with Chad. No, she
recalled definitely different upholstery. The padding had
stripes back then.

They'd probably succumbed to mildew years ago.

Liza found herself reluctant to sit down, though mildew
wasn't the reason.

There shouldn't be any traces of J.J. Pauncecombe's
ancient conquests, but who knows what Chad got up to out
here? The thought made Liza's lips quirk in a wry sort of
smile.

One thing was for sure. The quilted plastic upholstery
was too thin to serve as a hiding place for Chad's ill-gotten
gains.

Liza spotted a smaller pillow, the sort of thing you
might stick under your head while swinging in a hammock
on a long summer's day.

Who'd snooze on that bench? she found herself wondering. *It would be like taking a nap in a tomb.*

Still, wondering what kind of view she'd get out the
doorway, she plumped down onto the small pillow—and
got right back up as it jangled under her.

One hand went to rub her rear end while the other went
for that deceptive-looking cushion. Oh, there was some
padding, but there was also something metallic—in fact, a
whole bunch of metallic somethings—inside.

Taking it into the light from the doorway, Liza discovered one end of the cushion had apparently been opened and
then sewn up, not very expertly. She quickly unraveled the
stitches, plunged her hand inside, and came out with a huge
assortment of keys—hundreds of them—on several rings.

Each key had a three-digit number engraved on the
head. And as Liza jingled her way through them, she discovered they all began with the digit 1.

For a moment she began to get excited. *Maybe we didn't
need the whole row or column,* she thought. *Maybe it was
just the first three digits.*

But as she sorted through the jingling collection, that

first flush of enthusiasm diminished. Some of the keys had 0s in their ID numbers, so there couldn't be a direct connection between them and Chad's sudoku. And even if there were, how could she tell where the matching locks were?

Could they be for safe-deposit boxes? A key collection this big suggested hundreds of banks—like a bank for every town from Allentown to Albany.

Although each ring held a different variety of keys, the keys on each ring were almost identical.

Who would rent out whole sections of boxes in a safe-deposit vault? Liza asked herself skeptically. *And how could you mail stuff to them?*

She was close—she knew it the way she knew when she was almost at the point of cracking a tough sudoku, when finding one more complicated pattern like a swordfish would reduce the number of remaining clues until the simplest techniques would yield a solution. There had to be a connection between the nine-digit numbers in Chad's puzzles and the three-digit numbers on the keys, a step Liza was missing . . .

Mail, she thought.

Chad had posted the stolen cash. So there had to be a mail connection with the nine-digit numbers. She and Michael had eliminated zip codes. They couldn't be plain addresses.

So how could I hide an address in nine numbers? Liza asked herself.

She slowly smiled. No, the question was how had *Chad* managed to do that job?

Slipping her fingers through the key rings, Liza jingled her way back to her car. Once there, she dumped the keys and retrieved the manila envelope full of puzzles. Then she dialed the number for Ted Everard's cell phone.

He answered, but sounded kind of frustrated. "Liza? This isn't exactly a good time. I'm trying to get some information from Orem Whaley and my other new friends here at the elections office—"

"I have one more thing I'd like you to ask them, please,"

she interrupted. "The name and address connected with voter ID"—she ran a finger along one of the rows starting with 1—"number 153742896."

"What?" Ted's tone began to go from frustrated to harassed.

"Just see if that number is in their records," Liza said, "and we may find a ghost."

"Repeat that number," Ted told her.

Liza did, and Ted relayed it to the elections people he was meeting with. "Check your records for that voter ID," Liza heard him order. Apparently, he had reached the point where he wasn't in a mood to ask anymore.

"They're looking now," he reported. "Ah. They do have a record, for a Jane Fairfax."

"Emma," Liza muttered.

"No, *Jane* Fairfax," Ted corrected.

"Jane Austen," Liza tried to explain.

"No, Jane *Fairfax,*" Ted repeated, this time emphasizing the second name.

Liza sighed. "Jane Fairfax is a secondary character in Jane Austen's novel *Emma.* Chad seems to like using literary names. He used a character from *The Postman Always Rings Twice* as his alias to sign in at those motels—"

She cut herself off. "You must have an address, too."

"Number 179 Hillside Road," Ted told her.

"Great. Thanks, Ted. If this pans out, your troubles should be over."

Before Ted could ask any questions, she cut the connection and started the car.

Liza got back on the highway and retraced her route back to Maiden's Bay. She looped around downtown and her own neighborhood, heading for the hills—in this case, for the other end of Hillside Road. The part of the road she was familiar with had no development, and as she drove along, she quickly discovered that the far side was equally desolate.

In fact, the only building on the whole road was the glorified cinderblock shack with the faded CONVENIENCE sign in the front.

Liza got out of the car, stepped inside, and nodded hello to Mr. Patel. She stood for a moment, and then as a memory niggled at her, she walked with more confidence to the rear of the store, to the glass-doored freezer that held ice—and the back wall that held the rental mailboxes.

The plaques on the little metal doors started at 101. Liza ran along the rows till she found 179. Then she sorted through her three sets of keys. The first Key 179 didn't fit the lock. But the second did.

Heart pounding, Liza opened the little door. There was a little brown parcel inside! She really didn't think she'd be that lucky—Chad couldn't have sent money to all the names on his ghost voter rolls. Hands shaking a little, Liza removed the package addressed to Jane Fairfax.

For just a second, she hesitated. Did this count as tampering with the mail? But there wasn't a real Jane Fairfax, and she'd be bringing this straight to Sheriff Clements.

Liza closed and locked the mailbox and walked back out, giving Mr. Patel another cursory nod. She maintained a casual pace until she was outside the door. With those tiny windows, the store proprietor wouldn't be able to see her as she scuttled to her car, plopping the package on the front hood. Any attempt to be cool went out the window as her fingers excitedly fumbled with the wrappings.

She had to pay some attention to picking at the tape. Chad had sealed every seam as if he intended to make his package waterproof. Finally, though, Liza managed to get the damned stuff undone. The kraft paper had been wrapped several times around, so it took a little more effort before at last she exposed the contents of the brick-like little package.

Five packs of hundred-dollar bills had been rubber-banded together, creating a pile about two and a fraction inches wide, five and a fraction long, two and a half inches tall—and worth a cool fifty thousand dollars.

Liza took a deep breath at the sight of all that money.

Just as well she did, because a second later something slipped round her throat and pulled tight.

20

Whoever was trying to strangle Liza yanked heavily on the wire around her neck, dragging her back on her heels. She scrambled to get her feet under her, then straightened her legs with the next yank on the wire, ramming the back of her head into her attacker's face.

The choking pressure on her throat slackened, and Liza managed to twist loose. She turned, blinking stars from her eyes, and saw . . . Brandy Pauncecombe.

Her old high school rival had both hands to her face, but she was unmistakable—especially with that gold-scaled snake belt dangling from her fingers. That dropped to the dusty graveled parking lot, slipping away unnoticed as Brandy gingerly pressed and winced.

"By doze!" she exclaimed in a nasal voice. "You bitch, you broke by doze!"

Brandy's fingers curved into claws. "I'be godda kill you!"

She launched herself at Liza, who still had one hand at her throat as she tried to suck in air.

Liza barely had time to twist aside to avoid the attack. Brandy's perfectly manicured nails left a set of shallow scratches on Liza's cheek about an inch down from her right eye.

Brandy blundered past but pivoted round for another go. This time, Liza was ready for her. She didn't bother with this scratching stuff. She brought up her fists as she'd learned in childhood roughhousing with an older brother and his friends and from later self-defense courses.

When Brandy came at her this time, Liza brought her head down and her fist out in a solid jab that connected perfectly with Brandy's already damaged nose.

The pain must have been too much. Brandy's big brown eyes rolled back in her head, her knees buckled, and she dropped to the gravel pavement.

Liza waved her fists for a second more and then dropped them as she heard the distant scream of a siren come closer and closer. The police cruiser pulled up and Curt Walters came out, one hand on his holstered pistol, his eyes staring.

Well, he had a lot to look at, Liza had to admit—Brandy stretched on the ground, the open package of hundred-dollar bills scattered on the front hood of Liza's car, Liza's face . . .

Feeling a sting, Liza raised a hand to her cheek. Her fingers came away bloody. Immediately, her publicist persona took over. *I hope we can get some concealer on that before any cameras turn up.*

Meanwhile, Kurt walked carefully toward her, shaking his head. "You decked Brandy Pauncecombe," he said, his voice almost accusing. "And I missed it!"

Things moved quickly after that—again, Liza had the mental image of clinging to a rampaging machine. Sheriff Clements arrived, impounding the cash and Liza's collection of keys.

"How did you know to send—" Liza began.

"Got a call from Ted Everard," Clements cut her off. "Took him a little while to put things together—he had to call your husband."

That must have been fun, Liza thought.

"When he heard about the mailing and the puzzles, he connected them pretty quick to your request for a ghost voter address and got on the horn to me."

He sent a concerned glance at her throat. "Might have been better if we'd gotten here a little earlier."

Liza gingerly felt around, wincing. *Oh, great, bruises. That means more concealer, and I don't think Mr. Patel sells any.*

The sheriff used some of Liza's key collection to open a few more boxes and find additional brown paper parcels. Then he got on the phone to the postal authorities and got Liza and Brandy back to the Maiden's Bay substation—in different cars.

Liza gave a brief statement—or rather, a quick series of suggestions for the sheriff's upcoming press conference—while holding cold compresses to her scratches and bruises. Frankly, some of the stuff Clements pointed out didn't make either of them look good.

"So, moving in next door, the murderer had the perfect spot to maintain surveillance on you," he said severely. "And you were so wrapped up in your deductifying, you never noticed a silver BMW on your tail—or sitting on the other side of Patel's postage-stamp-sized parking lot."

"Ahhhhh, when you put it that way . . . ummmmmm . . . no," she admitted. "That's why we have to make the rest of this sound pretty good."

Shaking his head, the sheriff whisked her out the back door before the local news vans arrived.

Brandy's interrogation promised to run much longer and in an even less friendly fashion..

When she got home, Liza found Michael just about wearing a hole in the living room carpet with his pacing. His nervousness must have communicated itself to Rusty, because the dog trotted along in synch at Michael's right heel.

"Thank God," Michael muttered, wrapping Liza in a bearhug while Rusty capered around them. "When Ted Everard called and began asking about any other clues, it finally got through to me that you were out there following some sort of thread."

He took a deep breath. "And I know whenever that happens, somebody tries to kill you."

Michael pulled back, his eyes going wide as he took in the bandage on her cheek, the marks on her neck.

"It was Brandy," Liza tried to reassure him. "She tried the same thing on me that she did to Chad, except I broke her nose—twice."

He started to laugh. "Sounds like your high school fantasy come to life."

Liza grinned back at him. "I was ready to kick her butt all the way back to Maiden's Bay, except that the cops arrived."

Then she sobered. "The bad part is that I have to tell Mrs. H. that her new boarder will end up a guest of the state."

She tried to do the job over the phone, but Mrs. Halvorsen insisted on coming over to hear the whole story.

No sooner did Liza finish bringing both Michael and her neighbor up to date than she heard a knock at the kitchen door. She opened it to find Ted Everard standing outside.

"After what Bert Clements told me, I wanted to see you for myself." The look he gave to her hurts seemed more aggravated than afraid, but Ted just shook his head. "And the sheriff wanted me to let you in on what happened when he questioned Brandy Pauncecombe."

"Did she admit anything?" Liza asked.

He gave her a wry smile. "Brandy didn't have much of a choice. The marks that snake belt of hers made on your neck are an exact match for the marks on Chad Redbourne's throat."

Liza nodded, remembering how she'd seen the belt around Brandy's waist the afternoon of the murder. In fact, every time she'd seen Brandy since, the woman had worn the damned thing.

Maybe she was afraid to leave it out of her reach, she thought grimly. *Hell, she could even have worn it at night, since she apparently didn't share a bed with John Jacob.*

"In fact, once she started talking, it was hard to get Brandy to stop," Ted went on. "I guess our bumping into each other at Chad's office really must have shaken Redbourne up. Brandy told us that he called her out of the blue—something he wasn't supposed to do—and asked her to come to his place. She snuck in from a block away through the under-brush and found Chad waiting for her on the terrace. He started in immediately with some wild talk about being in too deep, ending up in jail with no help from his political cronies. He wanted them to leave town immediately, to go somewhere far from Killamook and the Pauncecombes."

"Doesn't sound like a bad idea to me," Michael said with a grin.

"Yeah, it was something they'd dreamed about," Ted replied, "but of course, they never had the kind of money it would take to make it happen. This time around, Chad got so wound up he began to stammer and shake."

"He used to do that sometimes in school," Liza said sadly.

Ted nodded. "That's what Brandy told us. She was just trying to stop him, to shock him out of it, when she looped her belt around his neck. She'd done it before—or so she claims."

"Chad could get scary when his words got stuck," Liza said. "But why wouldn't she just slap him? I guess he never got to the part about financing their escape—or Brandy couldn't understand it."

"By dumb luck, she managed to pull a commando move." Michael looked hard at Liza. "And it's just dumb luck that it didn't work on you."

Liza ignored the comment, thinking back to some-thing else Ted had said days ago, about how someone her size—or Brandy's, for that matter—could have staged the phony suicide scene in the Grotto.

"So she couldn't revive him, set up the scene to look like a suicide, then checked the house and found the suit-case. She frantically put everything where it was supposed to go, snuck out, and tried to go on with life as normal."

Michael picked up the narrative. "But life didn't stay normal. All sorts of dirt got stirred up about the Killamook machine, not to mention John Jacob and J.J. Then the whole story about the money came out, and the infighting began."

"I wonder how Brandy felt when she heard what Chad had done to help them get away," Liza said.

"According to Clements, she was crying a lot by then," Ted told her.

"Probably practicing for convincing the jury to let her off," Michael observed.

"And why shouldn't she?" Mrs. H. suddenly demanded.

Michael blinked. "Play the jury?"

"No, get off." Mrs. Halvorsen's expression wavered between sympathy for Brandy and disgust for the Pauncecombes. "Living with that degenerate beast of a man—out skirt chasing, then apparently wearing himself out." She made a face. "Probably popping those little blue pills. And that son of his . . . well, the nut doesn't fall far from the tree."

"With a definite emphasis on nuts," Michael quipped.

"Or she could have been an opportunist who paid her pig of a husband in the same coin—bopping everything that moved—and feared one of her partners was going to crack, so she killed him to shut him up." Liza put a hand around her throat. "And she was willing to do the same thing to me as soon as I found Chad's money for her."

"That doesn't—" Mrs. H. broke off, suddenly abashed. "No, it *does* make sense, doesn't it, when you consider what a nasty, spiteful brat she was growing up. I'm sorry, dear. Those awful Pauncecombes got me going." She stopped again. "And she played up to me pretty well, didn't she?"

Ted glanced at his watch. "I guess the final verdict will depend on how she looks when she goes to court. Want to catch a preview? The perp walk is scheduled for any minute now."

They immediately adjourned to the television set. As the image came on, Ted began to laugh. "Oh, Liza, you did a job on her."

Flanked by a pair of deputies, Brandy Pauncecombe walked from the front of the Maiden's Bay City Hall to a car waiting to deliver her to the Killamook jail. She didn't exactly look like a femme fatale, not with a bandage on her nose and a pair of twin shiners.

It almost looks like one of those little masks you see on people in comic books, Liza thought. *Superhero or super-villain? I guess only the court will decide—and that will depend on how well she heals and how often she crosses her legs.*

Ted looked over at her. "Clements told me one other thing—you wanted no credit in this case."

Michael swung around from the TV. "What?"

"That's pretty much the same thing Ava said when I called her from the car," Liza admitted with a lopsided smile. "I said that while I gave some technical help with the sudokus, he made the connection with the postal boxes and turned up the keys."

"And how did you wind up getting attacked at the convenience store?" Michael asked skeptically.

"Luring Brandy out into the open," Liza replied with an innocent look. "There was a slight problem with the surveillance, but it came out all right in the end."

The phone rang, and Liza excused herself to answer it.

"Now what were you up to this time?" Michelle Markson wanted to know.

"Taking a backseat, for once," Liza replied. "I don't need another media circus right now. For one thing, I can't afford another two-week vacation to recover from it."

"So someone else will emerge from this whole fiasco as a celebrity," Michelle said.

"Sheriff Clements?" Liza burst out in surprise.

"No, that amazingly foul-mouthed old man. He's become quite a phenomenon on YouTube. Since the ResusaGen people are taking their program national, they thought he would make the perfect spokesperson. Apparently, they believe that such a . . . full-bodied response can be taken as proof of virility."

Liza laughed, and Michelle cut off the call. Maybe that was just as well. Liza wouldn't be able to ask how her partner had found out that particular tidbit about John Jacob Pauncecombe.

On second thought, maybe I wouldn't want to know, she thought.

Michael had followed her to the kitchen giving her a sidewise glance. "So now I know why you handed Clements the case with a polka-dot bow on top."

"That, and of course, I wanted him to win the election." Liza grinned at him. "I figured it wouldn't hurt to have friends in high places."

"He was your friend before," Michael pointed out.

"You're right," Liza said lightly. "Okay, that's it. I'm done with politics."

"I hope not," Michael told her, surprisingly serious.

Liza stared. "Why?"

"Because someone once said that politics is the art of the possible," Michael replied softly. "And I still hope that, between us, anything is possible."

Sudo-cues

Variety Is the Spice . . .

Written by Oregon's own leading sudoku columnist, Liza K

Let me express my personal opinion up front. I enjoy sudoku, and I'm happy to play the game by the rules that have now become classic. But I am aware that out in the fringes of Sudoku Nation, some folks have become bored with puzzle monogamy. So today we'll take a look at what variations these sudoku swingers are up to.

Does size matter? Well, you can work in miniature with a puzzle like Rukodoku, with a six-by-six matrix, filling in the rows, columns, and three-by-two "boxes" with the digits 1 through 6. Or you can go bigger, with grids of ten on a side, or fifteen, sixteen . . . I've even seen a monster 81-by-81 puzzle, where, yes, each line and column takes the numbers 1 through 81, as do the nine nine-by-nine subgrids. (In other words, one subgrid is equal to the usual sudoku puzzle.) It looked interesting, but I have to admit that although I enjoy sudoku, I'd like to do other things as well, such as eating, sleeping, and occasionally going to the bathroom.

Another way to spice up sudoku is, as our math-minded friends might say, to vary the constraints. Hmmm. Sounds kind of kinky, but what it actually means is simply changing the rules. In plain old sudoku, you use the numbers 1 through 9, under the constraints that each row, column, and box must contain all the digits without repetition. Slash sudoku keeps all these rules, but also extends the non-repetition constraint to one of the nine-space diagonals "slashing" across the puzzle. X-sudoku adds more constraints (kinky, kinky!), extending the exclusion rule to both diagonals.

For those who feel boxed in by sudoku society's traditional folkways, there's irregular sudoku, also called geometric or jigsaw sudoku. The usual row and column constraints still hold, but the subgrid boxes become nine-space "regions" in irregular shapes to be filled with the magic numbers.

Color sudoku also eliminates the usual boxes, replacing them with sets of nine spaces in different colors. Rows, columns, and color sets accept the nine digits with no repeats. It certainly requires a shift of mental gears and creates a sort of numerical modern art.

Odd and even sudoku adds a more monochromatic approach to the traditional sudoku grid. A number of the spaces (thirty-six, to be exact) are shaded. The regular sudoku rules hold, with the additional constraint that only even numbers have it made in the shade.

Folks have played with the shape of the puzzle, even going to the extent of solving related puzzles in 3-D, with three sudoku appearing on the visual facets of a cube. They've even stretched and twisted the grid to create toroidal sudoku, where the eighty-one spaces we know and love become the flat representation of a torus or donut. What we were taught to consider usual boundaries actually border one another, so that irregularly shaped regions (à la irregular sudoku) twist through space across what we could consider the "top," "bottom," or "sides."

Some don't care about size or constraints—they just want to bend their brains.

These folks do away with the famous phrase that always

accompanies any description of "vanilla" sudoku—"You don't need to do any math to solve this puzzle."

I've seen sudoku grids where each nine-space box gets an additional decoration for the twelve interior dividing segments—the signs for "greater than" (>) or "less than" (<) as an additional constraint in placing the magic digits.

Killer sudoku brings in computation, abandoning the traditional boxes for irregularly shaped "cages" where the enclosed digits must add up to a sum posted in one of the spaces.

Kakuro bills itself as a number crossword, with shaded and clear spaces. Here segments of the puzzle are filled not with letters, but with numbers (our old friends 1–9) so that their sums equal the "across" or "down" clue.

Then there's the newly ubiquitous kenken, where a grid is broken into cages (as in killer sudoku). But you have to obtain the posted result of the cage not merely by adding, but through a variety of math operations. What's next—logarithmic or cosine kenken? Or maybe the puzzlers will get in touch with their feminine sides and create barbiebarbies?

I haven't even touched on variants like word sudoku, where nine letters instead of digits get used, or domino puzzles, which affect pairs of spaces—I even stumbled across a two-player variant game using sudoku rules.

I have to admit, though, that the variant that most fascinates me doesn't change any of sudoku's traditional rules, but rather the symbols. Picture or image sudoku retires the homely digits we're so familiar with and replaces them with . . . well, just about anything. I've seen puzzles with toys, cars, posters, photos of hamsters (check it out on beckysweb.co.uk/sudoku/flickrsudoku.asp) and Hollywood babes (on yourhomeabroad.com/imdoku/adlin.lku.html).

Here's a sample of image sudoku. Given the nonpuzzle constraints of paper quality and size, I can't bring on the hunks or the babes. But I can offer some connection with the numbers you know and love.

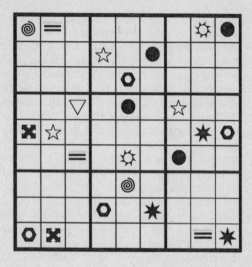

The faces may be different, but the rules remain the same. Looking across the middle set of boxes, you should quickly spot that the two black circles eliminate all but one space in the left-middle box, forcing the placement of a black circle, as shown.

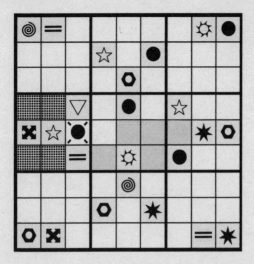

In that same row of boxes, white stars in the center-left and center-right boxes preclude the placement of any stars in the central box except for two spaces. The position of a third star in the top-center box eliminates one of those spaces, forcing the placement of a star as shown.

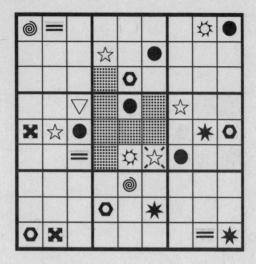

Looking up and down the center tier of boxes shows a similar situation. Hexagons in the top-center and bottom-center boxes allow only two spaces in the central box, and a hexagon in the right-center box cuts down those possible spaces to just one, as shown.

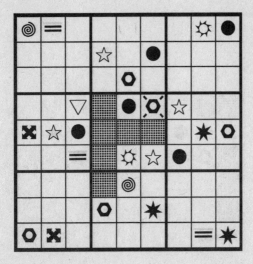

However, the placement of that hexagon creates another force play, this time in the middle-left box. The newly placed hexagon eliminates the two open spaces in the top row of the box while the hexagon in the lower-left box eliminated one of the two remaining possible open spaces. That forces the placement of another hexagon as shown.

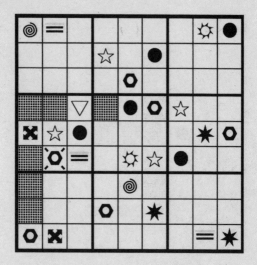

That's it for turning up any hidden singles. The next step is to start listing the candidates for each space, with an eye toward whittling those possibilities down.

Here's one of the drawbacks to doing image sudoku in a small puzzle format. If writing tiny numbers is a cause for eyestrain, drawing tiny symbols is completely ridiculous. Instead, I've opted to use the dot notation we've discussed in prior columns. I think you'll be able to hook up which dot represents which symbol.

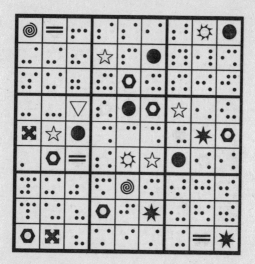

No sooner have we got everything listed than we spot
a space with only one possible candidate—a dark star—
for Column 1, Row 6, in the left-middle box, which we've
starred. This starts a chain reaction, deleting a dark star
·in Column 1, Row 4, two spaces above, establishing the
sunburst as the only possible candidate there (another star).
Furthermore, that deletes the possible sunburst next door
in Column 2, Row 4, leaving the spiral as the final candidate standing with another star.

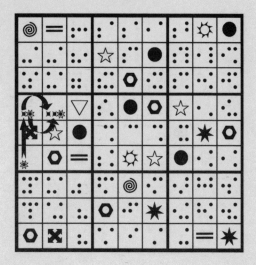

That actually solves out the entire box, as the next diagram shows.

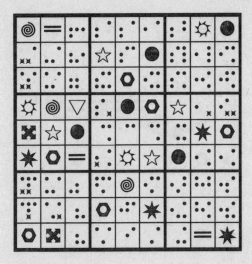

However, the chain reaction continues to rumble along. Look along Row 4 to the intersection with Column 8. The placement of a spiral six spaces back eliminates the spiral candidate here, leaving only the dot for the crossed arrows, which we've starred. One space farther along the row in Column 9, crossing out the arrow dot leaves only the candidate for the pair of bars, which we've starred.

But then, five spaces to the left in Row 4, Column 4, eliminating the representative for the bars leaves another single candidate—this time for the dark star. Guess what? That actually clears the whole row.

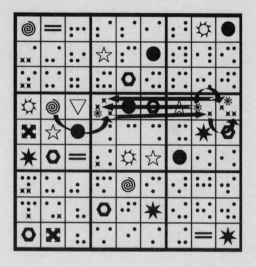

Are the aftershocks finished? Why, no! Here's a cleaned-up version of the puzzle:

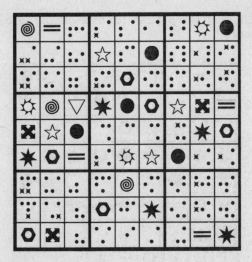

Moving up from Row 4 along Column 1, we encounter yet another single candidate at Row 2, which we've starred. That establishes the triangle in that space, eliminating three candidate spots in the upper-left-hand box and four more along the row.

Meanwhile, take a look at the last two spaces in Row 6—we've starred a naked pair sitting brazenly out there. (Okay, there are easier techniques to use, but they stood out, so I'm using them.) Since the spaces share candidate spots for the triangle and the spiral, those symbols can only be found there for the row. That means farther to the left at Row 6, Column 4, we can eliminate the dots representing the spiral and the triangle, leaving only the crossed arrows in control of the space. (As a matter of fact, this is the only remaining dot for that symbol in the row.)

That naked pair isn't done, however. The triangle-spiral duo prohibits the placement of those symbols anywhere in the middle-right-hand box. In this case that boils down to Row 5, Column 7. Crossing out the candidates for the

"taken" symbols leaves only one representative there—the
sunburst.

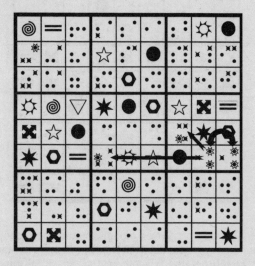

Here's where we stand after placing the appropriate
symbols in their proper places:

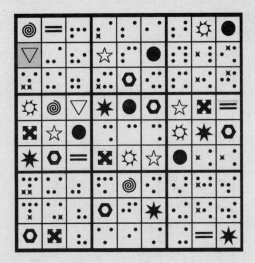

Clear away any remaining underbrush (there are six candidate dots to be crossed out), and you should find another lone candidate. Happy hunting!

I set out to make this a simple puzzle because of the shift in mental gears required from searching for symbols instead of numbers. It's like the time I decided to read *Pride and Prejudice* in translation to improve my Japanese. The story might be the same, but it looks a heck of a lot different!

Puzzle Solutions

Puzzle from pages 15 and 162

1	3	4	6	8	9	7	5	2
5	6	2	7	4	1	8	3	9
7	9	8	2	3	5	4	6	1
6	8	9	1	7	3	2	4	5
4	7	1	5	9	2	6	8	3
2	5	3	4	6	8	1	9	7
3	2	7	8	5	6	9	1	4
8	1	5	9	2	4	3	7	6
9	4	6	3	1	7	5	2	8

Puzzle Solutions

Puzzle from page 62

7	1	3	9	2	6	4	8	5
2	4	5	7	1	8	9	3	6
6	8	9	5	4	3	7	1	2
5	7	1	6	8	9	3	2	4
3	6	2	4	7	5	8	9	1
8	9	4	2	3	1	6	5	7
4	2	8	1	9	7	5	6	3
9	5	7	3	6	2	1	4	8
1	3	6	8	5	4	2	7	9

Puzzle from page 120

7	3	4	2	1	8	6	9	5
1	8	5	6	4	9	7	3	2
6	9	2	3	7	5	8	1	4
9	4	7	5	8	6	3	2	1
5	2	1	9	3	7	4	6	8
8	6	3	1	2	4	5	7	9
4	5	6	7	9	1	2	8	3
2	7	9	8	5	3	1	4	6
3	1	8	4	6	2	9	5	7

Puzzle from page 165

1	5	4	9	8	6	2	7	3
2	8	7	4	5	3	6	9	1
6	9	3	7	1	2	8	4	5
8	7	1	2	9	4	3	5	6
3	4	6	5	7	1	9	8	2
9	2	5	3	6	8	7	1	4
5	6	2	8	4	9	1	3	7
7	3	9	1	2	5	4	6	8
4	1	8	6	3	7	5	2	9

Puzzle from page 200

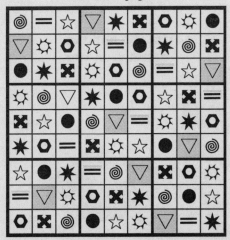

Praise for the Sudoku Mysteries

Sinister Sudoku

"Almost reads like an Agatha Christie . . . [A] very entertaining series . . . You do not need to be a fan of sudoku to enjoy the mystery, but if you are, you'll enjoy solving the puzzles and tips scattered throughout the story." —*CA Reviews*

"A wonderful addition to Ms. Morgan's Sudoku Mystery series! The narrative hits the ground running incorporating sudoku strategy with a treasure hunt and a tantalizing whodunit! I look forward to more!"
—*The Romance Readers Connection*

Murder by Numbers

"A fun read." —*Cozy Library*

"Kaye Morgan has written a cleverly constructed mystery that reflects the finely crafted sudoku puzzles that are included for fans to enjoy." —*The Mystery Gazette*

"Whether you are interested in sudoku or not, this mystery is fun and challenging." —*MyShelf.com*

Death by Sudoku

"The start of a great new amateur-sleuth series . . . Kaye Morgan is a talented storyteller who will go far in the mystery genre." —*The Best Reviews*

"The characters are likable . . . Sudoku plays an integral role, and puzzles are presented in various places for the reader to solve." —*Gumshoe Review*

"Puzzles and codes surround a vast pattern of murder . . . Sudoku lovers (like myself) will be delighted to see on the cover that this is the first of a series." —*Spinoff Reviews*

Berkley Prime Crime titles by Kaye Morgan

DEATH BY SUDOKU
MURDER BY NUMBERS
SINISTER SUDOKU
KILLER SUDOKU
GHOST SUDOKU